"I can't believe you remember that…"

Leah was quite clearly biting her tongue to control her laughter. "That was p-pretty hard to forget."

Silas took a deep breath. Thankful that the proverbial ice had been broken by his beverage mishap, he felt that this was the right time to apologize for being the menace that he'd been during his youth.

"Leah, I'm awful sorry about how I treated you when we were *kinner*. I never meant to actually hurt you." He looked her in the eyes as he expressed regret for his behavior. "If I'd only realized how much my words affected you, I would've never been so cruel."

"Okay" came Leah's soft voice from across the table.

"I promise you," he pressed on, reaching for her hand, "I will never let you down again."

Once again, he briefly considered how very easily he could develop a serious romantic interest in her. Her gentle ways and hardworking spirit were very attractive, as was her lovely face.

Silas had to admit the truth to himself… He had a crush on Leah.

Jackie Stef began immersing herself in Amish culture at a young age and wrote her first Amish story at eleven years old. When she's not busy writing, she enjoys photography, playing with her pets and exploring the back roads of Lancaster County. She lives in rural Pennsylvania and loves to spend time in nature.

Books by Jackie Stef

Love Inspired

Their Make-Believe Match

Bird-in-Hand Brides

Trusting Her Amish Rival

Visit the Author Profile page at LoveInspired.com.

Trusting Her Amish Rival

Jackie Stef

LOVE INSPIRED

INSPIRATIONAL ROMANCE

LOVE INSPIRED®
INSPIRATIONAL ROMANCE

Recycling programs
for this product may
not exist in your area.

ISBN-13: 978-1-335-59835-6

Trusting Her Amish Rival

Love Inspired
22 Adelaide St. West, 41st Floor
Toronto, Ontario M5H 4E3, Canada
www.LoveInspired.com

Printed in U.S.A.

But I say unto you, Love your enemies, bless them that curse you, do good to them that hate you, and pray for them which despitefully use you, and persecute you.
—*Matthew* 5:44

This book is dedicated to the strongest women that I know, Diane Stefanowicz and Emilie Peters. Your influences on my life are significant, and I'm blessed to know both of you.

Chapter One

Bird-in-Hand, Pennsylvania

"Leah, the first bus of the day just arrived. We better get out there to greet your customers."

Leah Fisher stood at the kitchen table packing a variety of fresh baked goods into two wooden crates. At her father Ezra's alert, she spun around and dashed to the nearby window. "*Ach*, th-they're early. My s-stand doesn't open for another fifteen minutes." Ever since her girlhood days, Leah had always been the anxious sort. If there was something to worry about, she would certainly find it. She had a stutter that worsened during times of stress, much to her embarrassment. "I haven't s-stocked any baked goods or v-vegetables yet," she huffed as she hurried back to the table to continue loading her crates with the pastries that she'd baked the previous evening.

Ezra chuckled and gave his graying beard a yank. "No need to fret, *dochder*. There are plenty of items for the tourists to browse through while you put these *appenditlich* pastries out for sale." He ambled toward the table and rested a hand on his daughter's slight shoulder. "It looks like they're already posing for pictures next to our buggy and petting that *hund* of yours."

Leah grinned at her father's mention of her Dalmatian, Willow, knowing that her canine companion was excitedly greeting their visitors with playful woofs. "*Jah*, I suppose th-there's lots to see on one's f-first visit to an Amish farm."

"That's for sure." Ezra peeked into one of the crates and swiped a red velvet whoopie pie with a mischievous smirk. "Since I'm helping you carry these crates and arranging your baked goods, I'll take one of these as payment for my services."

Leah feigned annoyance for only a moment, unable to hide her smile, her hazel eyes twinkling. "*Vell*, we b-better get out there before you gobble down so much that I w-won't have anything left to sell!"

Laughing heartily together, Leah and her father gathered up the crates and exited the large white farmhouse. They headed across the well-maintained lawn to Leah's roadside stand, which had been built just a few rooster steps from the house. It was a mild mid-September day in Lancaster County and the tourist season was still going strong. Leah knew she could still expect plenty of visitors during each day that her business was open, at least until late October.

Leah fondly recalled setting up a folding table at the edge of her driveway, just after her fifteenth birthday, when she only intended to sell a few loaves of her fluffy homemade bread. Now, a building that resembled a miniature cottage stood where that single folding table had been set up just over five years ago. The quaint little store was where Leah spent most of her time, and it kept her rather busy. Alongside her pastries, she consigned seasonal produce from her mother's garden, jams and jellies canned by her eldest sister, Martha, and homemade crafts from her closest friend, Fern Lapp. "Leah's Countryside Cupboard" had become a popular spot for locals to pick up a tasty snack. It was also a true hidden gem that tourists were thrilled to discover as they explored the peaceful backroads of Amish Country.

Leah's parents and older sibling had hoped that becoming a business owner would improve her confidence and chase away the nagging voice of her anxiety, though Leah was never able to fully quiet her worries. Her stuttering could be mortifying, as it had been during her childhood, but thankfully none of her customers ever chuckled or made snide remarks when she stumbled over her words. She longed to overcome her anxiety and speech problem, but some days, it felt like a dream that would never come true. For now, she would focus on the peaceful life she led, remembering to pray regularly that nothing would come crashing into her world to disrupt it.

After the crates were unloaded, Ezra wished his daughter a pleasant day and headed toward the barn to continue his chores. Leah scampered behind her battery-powered cash register and cheerfully assisted customers with their purchases while Willow wandered around the shop and ensured every customer was greeted. The steady flow of shoppers lasted throughout the morning, and Leah only had a chance to catch her breath after two more tour buses and several carloads of visitors had leisurely browsed through her wares. Deciding to take advantage of the quiet moment, she found her watering can in a small closet that was located behind the counter. She stepped outside and sprinted to the hand-powered water pump. With a few quick pumps, she filled the can with crystal-clear water then rushed back to-ward the roadside stand to tend to the mums she had for sale.

When she rounded the corner of the small building, she noticed a lone horse and buggy at the hitching rail in the tiny parking lot. It wasn't uncommon for a fellow Amish friend or neighbor to come for a visit. Sometimes they stopped by the small store to pick up a gift for a friend or a scrumptious dessert.

Maybe I'll close the shop for a half hour and invite them to have lunch with me, Leah thought as she headed for the shop's entrance with a spring in her step.

A tall Amish man dressed in a violet shirt, black trousers suspenders, and a straw hat stood at the counter, rummaging through the basket of whoopie pies that was placed near the cash register. Hearing the small bell above the door jingle when Leah entered the shop, the man turned to face her.

"Guder mariye, Leah!"

Leah's smile morphed into a scowl faster than the flapping of a hummingbird's wings. Silas Riehl was the last person that she wanted in her shop. During their childhood days at the one-room schoolhouse on Stumptown Road, Silas had tormented Leah relentlessly about her stutter. From the first day of first grade to their last day of eighth grade, he had been downright cruel. His teasing had been so severe that it had caused Leah to develop severe anxiety. She had often cried and became nauseous before it was time to go to school. When Leah no longer had to interact with Silas every day in their teenage years, her confidence had slowly improved. At the age of sixteen, she joined the Amish church and maintained a pious reputation. Silas, on the other hand, experienced a wild *rumspringa*. Instead of owning a cell phone and wearing *Englisch* clothes, Silas threw wild parties involving heavy drinking, and he even had a few interactions with the local police. After a few years of shenanigans, Silas renounced his untamed ways, joined the Amish church, and now lived a respectable life. The community seemed to have welcomed him back with open arms, but Leah had tremendous doubts that Silas had truly matured. How could someone who tormented a stuttering child change that much? Even after all these years, she knew she would never be able to get over how poorly Silas had treated her.

Ignoring Silas's greeting, she nervously smoothed the wrinkles out of her black cape-apron. She scurried across the shop and took her familiar post behind the counter. "How can I help y-you?"

Silas offered her a friendly smile, which almost caused Leah to roll her eyes. "I'm looking for some mint chocolate whoopie pies. They're my favorite, and the bakery in town was sold out. You have any?"

Leah held back a sigh. She didn't have any mint chocolate whoopie pies for sale, but she'd packed a week-old one with her lunch. That flavor was her favorite as well, and she'd been looking forward to enjoying it with her lunch. "I have one in the c-cooler," Leah answered curtly. She bent and reached into the cooler that rested in a nook under the counter. "It's f-from last week's b-batch. If you p-prefer something else, there are s-several other f-flavors to choose from," she stumbled over her words, feeling her face flaming with embarrassment at the worsening of her stutter. Although they were both adults and she was no longer afraid of Silas, his presence was still enough to make her nervous. Her anxiety affected her stuttering and that gave birth to a regular vicious cycle.

"*Ach*, I don't mind. I'll take the chocolate-mint one," Silas replied as he accepted the whoopie pie with one hand and reached into his pocket to retrieve his wallet with the other.

Leah held up her hand to stop him. "No ch-charge."

Silas's eyebrows drew together above his ocean-blue eyes. "That's *oll recht*." He retrieved a bill from his wallet. "You're running a business here, *jah*?"

"I w-won't ch-charge you for a week-old whoopie p-pie." Leah's face felt so hot that it nearly made her eyes water.

"Denki." He grinned boyishly and then glanced around the shop. "I've never been in here before. This is a great place you have. Do you get lots of customers?"

Leah groaned inwardly. Making conversation with Silas felt like getting stung by a bee. *"Jah*, especially in the s-summer and f-fall." She looked down at the counter and swiped away some imaginary crumbs. Anything to keep from making eye contact with her childhood tormenter.

"Sounds about right, since that's the busiest time for the tourists." Silas tore away the plastic wrapping from his whoopie pie and took a bite. "This is tasty! Do you make all the pastries here?"

Leah nodded, unable to muster up a verbal answer.

After he finished the last bite, Silas's mouth opened as if he was going to say something more, but he just scanned the shelves once again. Several painful seconds passed before he spoke up again. "I better get going. See you around." With that, Silas headed out the door.

Leah exhaled so forcefully that she felt faint. Had she been holding her breath since she recognized that it was Silas standing in her shop? She hurried to the nearby open window and watched him plod to his waiting buggy. Once he backed up his horse and turned it to leave the parking lot, Leah exited the shop and located the watering can once more. She was glad to have this task to occupy herself. Watering her thirsty flowers and getting fresh air would help calm her nerves.

As Leah watered each plant and plucked off the occasional dead leaf, she heard the clip-clop of horse's hooves and the rumble of buggy wheels approaching. Another customer? She turned to see who was pulling in, but the parking lot was empty. As the sound of the buggy drew closer, she turned toward the driveway that led to the house and barn. There was Silas, sitting proud as a peacock in his open buggy, headed toward the farm! He waved politely as he went by, his sandy-blond bowl-cut hair disheveling itself in the breeze.

Leah's mouth fell open as shock coiled through her veins. Why was Silas headed toward her home instead of back out to the road? Had he started to daydream and forgotten to control his horse? She felt her heart begin to pound, a combination of irritation and uncertainty fueling its frenzied beating.

Forcing herself to calm down, she tried to think rationally. If Silas was headed for the barn, he was most likely seeking out her father. But what would Silas need with her *daed*? Leah shuddered uncomfortably as she went back to watering the colorful mums. She'd find out soon enough. Hopefully, Silas was just visiting her *daed* to share some community news or perhaps ask for some small favor, and it would be the end of his presence around her family's farm, Lord willing.

"That went well," Silas Riehl chided himself as his rig approached the Fishers' enormous white barn. His horse and buggy ride business, Riehl's Buggy Rides, had become so popular with tourists that he was thinking of expanding the available tour routes, and the idea of bringing guests to a working Amish farm and business was appealing. The plain yet majestic Fisher farm located on Stumptown Road was the perfect place for those looking for a quiet getaway in Amish country. Of course, before he could offer his customers a farm tour and a stop at an Amish business, he'd have to get permission from the Fisher family.

Silas pulled his buggy up to the hitching rail adjacent to the barn and hoped that his interaction with Leah's father would go more smoothly than his conversation with Leah. He'd intended to propose the notion of partnering their businesses during their interaction, but he'd chickened out as soon as he saw how tense she looked. Leah was visibly uncomfortable being near him, trembling and refusing to look him in the eye.

She had every right to be nervous, Silas reminded himself as he set the buggy's brake and hopped to the ground. If he could take back the years of cruel jokes and mean-spirited comments that he'd made during his childhood, he would do so in a heartbeat.

He'd been a carefree youngster who never considered the consequences of his actions, and as a teenager he'd been wild and reckless, often drinking in excess. Silas had carried on like this until he crashed the used pickup truck he'd purchased into a tree on his grandparents' property after a night filled with heavy drinking. After seeing the disappointment in his grandparents' wrinkled faces and getting a very powerful talking-to from his grandfather, Silas changed his untamed ways. By his twentieth birthday, he joined the Amish church and established his business. His parents could finally be proud of their only child. Now, three years later, it seemed like no one remembered the obnoxious young man he used to be, except for Leah Fisher.

What a shame it was that Leah still saw him as an enemy! Silas hadn't spoken to Leah since the day they graduated from the nearby one-room schoolhouse. He'd seen her from afar at the biweekly church gatherings, but until today he'd never realized what a stunning woman she had blossomed into. With Leah's piercing hazel eyes and dark chestnut hair, it was a wonder that some eligible bachelor hadn't snatched her up to be his wife. More importantly, she was hard-working and kind, which meant that she was well-liked within their community. Silas had noticed several of his male peers approaching and flirting with Leah at youth gatherings, and through the grapevine, he'd learned that she'd gone on several dates, but nothing serious ever seemed to come from those outings. Maybe the fellows got cold feet after seeing what an independent woman she was. Or, could it be that Leah was exceptionally picky when it came to courting? Perhaps she was hoping to court someone specific.

If she was purposely staying single and holding out for someone special, that special someone certainly wasn't him. Silas huffed to himself as he surveyed the Fisher barnyard in search of Ezra. Maybe if he hadn't terrorized Leah so much when they were children, they could at least be on friendly terms, which would certainly have made today's mission easier.

Deciding not to fret over the past, Silas entered the barn in his search for Ezra. After a few moments of wandering through different areas of the structure, Silas finally found him spreading some fresh pine bedding in an empty horse stall.

"Hello, Ezra," Silas greeted Leah's father. He mustered up the friendliest smile he could, just in case the middle-aged man held a grudge against him for harassing his daughter in their childhood days.

He felt instant relief when Ezra looked up from his work and smiled at him. "*Guder mariye*, Silas! What can I do for you?"

Silas suppressed the need to deeply exhale. Ezra seemed welcoming and not annoyed by his sudden appearance on the property. He glanced down as an orange barn cat rubbed against his leg. "I wanted to get your thoughts on an idea I had for my buggy rides business," he answered as he reached down to pet the friendly feline. "I have more customers than ever before, and I only have two ride options for them to choose from. I offer a three-mile ride and a six-mile ride. I think it might be nice to offer customers the option to have a ride with a stop at an Amish farm and business."

"And you were thinking about bringing folks here?"

"*Jah*, I thought maybe I or one of my drivers could bring people here to see the animals and how we get our work done without electricity." Silas scratched the cat's ears as the volume of its purring increased. "Of course, we would respect your privacy and wouldn't go near the house. I thought I could share some of the profits from the farm tours with your family if you were agreeable to the idea."

Ezra leaned against his pitchfork. "If it's just around the barn, I don't have a problem with that. I appreciate your offer to share profits, but that's your money to keep. If you want to bring folks to tour the farm, you're welcome to do so."

"Can I also take guests to Leah's shop? I'm sure the tourists would love the chance to buy something Amish-made," Silas suggested as he straightened up to his full height.

Ezra bobbed his head in agreement as he went back to spreading the fresh bedding. "*Jah*, that would be *gut*, but you'll need to also see if this arrangement is *oll recht* with Leah."

"Of course, I'll make sure I run this past her before I start bringing folks here," Silas agreed wholeheartedly. A sense of nervousness flitted through his chest. He'd obtained Ezra's approval but gaining Leah's consent might prove to be a battle.

If only I'd dared to ask her about this plan earlier, Silas reprimanded himself. He couldn't go seek her out at her shop a second time that same day, not after the cold reception she'd given him earlier. It would have to wait for now.

Ezra asked Silas to wait a week or two before bringing tourists to the farm so he could spruce up the barn and repaint Leah's shop, and Silas agreed. After a few moments of small talk, Silas bid Ezra farewell and headed back to his waiting horse and buggy.

Although his visit to the Fishers' farm had only been partially successful, Silas couldn't help but grin. Winning Leah over would undoubtedly be a challenge, but it was a challenge he would have to face for the sake of his business.

Chapter Two

Later that evening, Leah glanced over her shoulder at the dinner table while she washed the dinner plates. Her father was the only remaining family member still seated at the table following the meal, as he finished up a second helping of her peanut butter pie. Anxiously looking for an opportunity to speak with him privately, Leah had urged her mother and four younger siblings to relax while she cleaned up. Only her ten-year-old sister, Sarah, refused Leah's polite coaxing to skip the chore. The talkative child went on and on about her day at the schoolhouse as she dried and put away the dishes that Leah scrubbed clean, though most of her stories had fallen on Leah's unconsciously deaf ears.

"Teacher Katie says that we'll get report cards on Friday, and I know I'll have straight

A's," the girl chirped as she stood on her tip-toes to place a dry plate back in the cupboard. "She said that anyone who gets straight A's can have an extra hour of recess every day next week."

Though Leah had difficulty focusing on the conversation with her kid-sister, she was pleased to hear the child's news. "Th-that's *wunderbaar*, Sarah. I know you've b-been working hard." She peeked over her shoulder again and was relieved to see that her father hadn't finished his pie and was still seated at the table.

Turning her attention back to Sarah, Leah gestured a soapy hand toward the window. "It's a *sch-schee* evening. Why don't you go do your h-homework outside in the f-fresh air?"

Sarah shook her head. "I'd rather stay here and help you."

Leah smiled down at the child who always seemed very eager to please. "This chore is almost d-done and I can finish up here on my own. G-go finish your homework so you can keep up those s-straight A's."

Sarah finally agreed and dried her hands on her brown chore dress before dashing out of the kitchen. When she was sure that her sister was out of earshot, Leah reached for a dirty plate and dunked it into the sudsy water as she asked the question that she'd been fretting over all day.

"*Daed*, I saw Silas Riehl headed toward the b-barn around lunchtime. What did he w-want?"

Ezra forked a hunk of pie into his mouth, prolonging Leah's apprehension. "He asked if he could bring customers from his buggy ride business to our farm for tours."

Leah gasped and dropped the plate into the sudsy water. "Wh-what did you say?" she asked as she whirled around to face her father, fearing that she'd heard him incorrectly. Surely, Silas wasn't planning on making regular appearances here, in the sacred peacefulness of the place she called home!

Ezra looked up from his dessert as a concerned expression crossed his tanned face. "*Jah*, he wants to offer his customers rides to an Amish farm and business." He used the side of his fork to slice another bite-size piece of his pie. "Didn't he speak to you about this? I told him that he'd have to make sure it was *oll recht* with you as well."

Leah's mouth fell open and hung for a moment. "He c-certainly d-didn't!" She felt her cheeks begin to burn. "He came into the sh-shop and wanted a whoopie p-pie, and th-then he left." Leah turned back to the sink and began rewashing the dish. She didn't want her father to see the horror that she was sure was written all over her face. It was embarrassing that her childhood bully still had such a negative effect on her.

Ezra grunted around the last mouthful of pie, using his fork to scrape up every last crumb. "That's odd, but I'm sure he'll get around to speaking with you. The buggy rides won't start coming here for another week or two anyway."

Leah started to say something, but she became so flustered and tongue-tied that she had to stop to take a deep breath. "I don't w-want Silas b-bringing folks here."

She heard her father's wooden chair creak as he stood, followed by the sound of his work boots clomping across the floor. "Why not? I figured you'd welcome the extra business," he said as he handed Leah his plate and fork.

Leah dropped the items into the water and let them sink to the bottom. She placed her trembling hands against the counter and leaned on it, feeling too weak to stand. This was too much to process and now her stomach was doing somersaults.

"Leah," Ezra persisted, placing his hand on his daughter's cheek and turning her face toward him. "Tell your *daed* what's got you so upset."

She heaved a sigh as her shoulders drooped. "Honestly, *Daed*, the th-thought of Silas sh-showing up here frequently m-makes me sick! Don't you r-remember how he bullied me when we w-were *kinner*?" She shuddered, fighting the hot tears that burned to be released. "How c-could you welcome someone like S-Silas to our home?"

"*Ach*, Leah, my sweet *maedel*," Ezra cooed with a tilt of his head. "I didn't know you still felt so strongly about Silas."

Leah shrugged, unsure of how to reply.

After using his thumb to wipe away his grown daughter's tears, Ezra motioned toward the table. "*Kumme* sit with me." Leah followed her father to the table and took a seat adjacent to him. He allowed her a few moments to compose herself before he spoke again. "Silas seemed *naerfich* when we talked today. No doubt he remembers treating you poorly."

"He sh-should be *naerfich*. He was d-downright cruel to m-me," Leah hiccupped, dabbing her eyes with her damp apron. "Wh-why does he have to bring t-tourists here?"

"He said he wanted to offer his customers the option to tour an Amish farm and shop at an Amish business. Leah's Countryside Cupboard is the closest Amish-run business to Riehl's Buggy Rides, and it's located on a farm, so his plan makes sense, ain't so?"

Leah harrumphed and crossed her arms over her chest. "That doesn't m-make me feel any better. He's a *baremlich* p-person. I don't w-want anything to do with him."

Ezra's eyebrows climbed high on his forehead. "Is that my sweet Leah talking like that?"

Her father's question caught Leah off guard and pierced right through her heart. Her cheeks flushed again, but this time from guilt.

Ezra sighed and combed his fingers through his beard. "I remember the days when you came home from *schul* with tears streaming down your cheeks after Silas had teased you about your stutter. It was wrong of him, and it was shameful for him to have carried out such a wild *rumspringa*." He reached for Leah's soft hand and held it in his callused one. "But Silas renounced his sins and joined our church, committing to follow *Gott*. He's been a decent person ever since. If the Lord can forgive him, isn't it our duty to forgive Silas as well?"

Leah stared down at her bare feet on the linoleum floor, unable to look her father in the eye. "I g-guess I'll have to t-try my best."

Ezra grinned, releasing Leah's hand and tapping the tip of her nose as he often did when she was a child. "Let's give Silas a chance. I'm sure he'll approach you to discuss partnering your businesses." Ezra pushed his palms against his knees and stood with a muted grunt. "Besides, you are both grown now." His eyes twinkled as he gave the smile of a loving, patient parent. "Trust in *Gott* and don't give in to your anxiety, Leah. I know you can handle this, with *Gott*'s help."

Leah thanked her father for his comforting words and then returned to the sink. As she dried the last dish and returned it to the stack in the cabinet, she contemplated her father's words. Struggling to believe his sentiment, Leah doubted that Silas could ever change. She, however, had grown, just as her father had described. Determined not to be intimidated by Silas for a moment longer, Leah decided to open her shop late tomorrow. She would visit Silas right after breakfast and confront him about his plan since he wasn't decent enough to approach her first.

Shortly after breakfast the next morning, Silas busied himself with completing chores before Riehl's Buggy Rides would open to customers. The small, popular attraction was located at the edge of the Riehl farm, which allowed Silas to house and care for all ten of his draft horses on-site. He'd considered allowing visitors to tour his father's small farm, but he'd quickly nixed the idea knowing that there was far more to see at the Fisher farm, as well as at Leah's Countryside Cupboard. Though his family's farm might not be as interesting to tourists as the Fishers', Silas did his best to maintain the small area where he welcomed his customers. That morning he washed down the tables near the small but frequently used picnic area. Then he swept the wooden floor of the quaint, white gazebo that overlooked the meadow where his horses grazed contentedly. When that chore was done, he moved to the small shed that he ran the business from, where guests could choose and pay for their ride. He entered the shed, slid the window open, then located the small cardboard box hidden behind the counter. With the box in hand, he headed to the display of brochures for local restaurants and attractions that hung on the side of the shed. As he restocked the pamphlets, he yawned for what felt like the hundredth time since he'd been tidying up.

"No wonder I'm exhausted," Silas muttered to himself, fighting off yet another yawn. After yesterday's awkward encounter with Leah, he'd spent the rest of the day and most of the night worrying about how he would approach her to discuss partnering their businesses. "If only I'd gotten it over with yesterday. What a coward."

"You talking to yourself, boss?" Silas turned to see Ivan Schrock approaching with his usual wide grin. Tall, lanky, witty Ivan was Silas's close friend and best employee, and he could always count on Ivan to crack a joke.

"I wish you wouldn't call me boss. It makes me uncomfortable," Silas replied with a roll of his eyes and a crooked smile.

Ivan ran his thumbs under his suspenders and gave them a snap. "Sure, Mr. Riehl, anything you say. Which horses would you like me to get hitched up for rides today?"

Silas shook his head and chuckled, comforted by his friend's familiar sense of humor. "Lightning and Thunder had a day off yesterday, so if you could get them hitched to carriages one and two, that would be great." He turned back to his display of brochures, filling in the last spot with pamphlets for the Bird-in-Hand Family Restaurant, one of his favorite places. When he didn't hear Ivan's heavy footsteps departing, Silas glanced back at his friend. "Everything *oll recht*?"

"I'm about to find out," Ivan replied with another snap of his suspenders. "How'd it go yesterday at the Fishers'?"

"It didn't," Silas answered quietly as he stepped back into the shed.

Ivan's dark eyebrows furrowed. "Why not? I thought you spent your lunch break going over to talk to Leah. Wasn't she at the road-side stand?"

Silas shrugged in disappointment as he returned the brochure box to its spot. "I did go there, but I only talked with Ezra. I was too *naerfich* to talk to Leah."

Truthfully, he was somewhat ashamed of himself. Leah was a petite little thing, yet Silas had lost his nerve, which had taken him several days to build up, when they were face-to-face. Was he ashamed of his boyhood bullying habit, or was his lack of confidence triggered by his sudden realization that Leah was now a gorgeous young woman, like a lovely late-blooming sunflower?

The sounds of horses' hooves trotting and buggy wheels crunching against the gravel interrupted Silas's thoughts.

Ivan glanced around the side of the shed to see who had arrived. He issued an amused snort as he turned back toward Silas. "*Vell*, there's no time like the present!"

"What do you mean?"

"Leah's out there tying her horse to the

hitching rail. Looks like she came to talk to you."

Silas felt his heart jump into his throat. In his wildest dreams, he would have never imagined Leah willingly coming to visit him. She clearly couldn't stand him, and of course, she had every right to feel that way. He cautiously peeked out the open window but quickly shrunk back when Leah shot him a fuming glare.

"She's probably here to chew me out." Silas slapped his hand to his forehead and rubbed small circles into his skin. "Her *daed* probably told her about my plan, and now she's upset that I didn't mention it to her too."

"That could very well be," Ivan agreed with a shrug. "But Leah's always been as sweet as blueberry pie. Even if she has a bee in her bonnet, she'll get over it if you apologize."

"That's easy for you to say. You never bullied her when we were *kinner*," Silas replied quietly as he watched Leah march up the sidewalk like she was on a mission. Even with the obvious scowl across her lips, she was as beautiful as a winter sunset.

Leah's fiery expression softened when her eyes landed on Ivan. More than likely, Ivan's cheerful grin would take her fury down a few notches.

"Hello, I-Ivan," she greeted him pleasantly. "*Wie b-bischt?*"

"Doing real *gut*, and so was the pie my *mamm* picked up from your roadside stand yesterday. We had it after dinner, and I enjoyed two slices," Ivan responded, giving his stomach a few pats.

"I'm g-glad you liked it," she said with a warm smile that quickly turned icy when she glanced toward Silas.

Ivan clapped his hands together, causing Silas to flinch. "We're opening for business soon, so I better get the horses ready for the day. Nice to see you, Leah!" Ivan offered Leah a winning smile, then turned on his heels and scurried toward the Riehls' barn.

Silas watched Ivan's retreating form and groaned inwardly. It would have been a comfort to have Ivan's support during this confrontation with Leah. He turned to face her and felt his blood pressure rise when he took in her grimace, though her vibrant hazel eyes were a lovely distraction from her scowl.

With the grace of a hurricane, Leah stomped toward the shed, then up to the window. She looked Silas up and down as if sizing up her opponent.

"I guess your *daed* told you about my plans to bring my buggy rides to your farm."

Leah crossed her arms over her chest, keeping her blazing gaze on Silas. "*Jah*, he t-told me, s-since he's a d-decent person!"

Her words stung Silas like a horsefly bite. He so badly wanted to start their business relationship off on the right foot, but it was too late for that now. "I'm awful sorry, Leah. I was planning to talk to you since I'd like to bring tourists to the roadside stand, but—"

"B-b-but you went b-behind my back instead!" Leah's eyes narrowed into thin slits and the tip of her nose began to turn pink.

Even though her sharp tone sounded like an angry junkyard dog, Silas couldn't help but grin. She certainly wasn't the little girl he'd picked on all those years ago, though her stature was still quite small.

"Y-you have a lot of n-nerve," she spat at Silas, pointing an accusing finger in his direction. "You went b-behind my back, and th-then have the gall to s-smile about it!"

Silas bit down hard on his tongue to prevent himself from snapping back at Leah. She was still seeing him as the mischievous boy he'd once been, not the hard-working, sincere man he'd become. Maybe his idea to take his customers to the Fisher farm was a mistake since he would have to interact with Leah every day. He balled his fingers into fists out of frustration. "Listen, if you would just give me a chance to—"

"To wh-what? To t-torment me again?"

Silas sharply inhaled, but before he could respond the sound of car doors slamming caught his attention. His first customers of the day, a group of four older *Englisch* ladies chatted excitedly as they approached the shed to choose and pay for their ride.

"*Wilkumme*, ladies," Silas cheerfully greeted his guests with a smile and a wave. "Come for a buggy ride?"

"We sure did," replied one of the women, her eyebrows raising high above the lenses of her stylish sunglasses. "This place comes highly recommended."

Silas grinned until he caught a glimpse of Leah, who was still staring him down like an angry bull. It wasn't good to have her here, looking so unfriendly, which his customers would surely notice.

Thinking fast, Silas motioned to the sign behind him. "We currently offer two different tour routes to choose from."

The tourist ladies chatted among themselves, trying to decide on which ride to take, but Silas was more focused on Leah, who stood off to the side, looking madder than a hornet. What was he supposed to do? Should he ignore Leah, which would only make her more upset, or inconvenience his customers by pulling Leah aside to privately continue their conversation?

"We'd like to take the six-mile ride," one of the *Englisch* women announced as the ladies reached into their purses to pay for their tour.

Silas accepted their payments and was handing them their change when he finally breathed a sigh of relief. The sound of horse hooves and Ivan's chipper whistling were approaching. Now that Ivan was back from the barn with one of the carriages, he could take the customers on their tour while Silas dealt with Leah.

"Ivan, these ladies are going on the six-mile ride. If you can take them now, I'll get the second buggy ready in a few minutes."

Ivan agreed and welcomed the group of tourists, asking them to follow him to the hitching rail, where they could safely enter the buggy. When Ivan and the customers were out of earshot, Silas turned to Leah. "Would you please wait for me in the gazebo? I need to see these customers off on their ride, then I'll meet you there."

Leah tapped her foot impatiently and chewed on her lower lip as if mulling over his request. Finally, she wordlessly stomped off toward the gazebo.

Silas let out a pent-up sigh through pursed

lips. He'd avoided making a bad impression in front of his customers, but he knew the battle to win Leah's trust was far from over. He took off his hat and ran his hand through his wavy blond hair, unintentionally ruffling his locks to match his current emotions. Taking a few moments to collect his thoughts before facing Leah again, Silas sent up a quick prayer.

Lord, I know it's Your will for us to not have any enemies. If I'm ever to patch things up with Leah, I'm going to need Your help.

Chapter Three

Leah nervously paced back and forth across the creaking wooden floorboards of the gazebo, wringing her hands together so tightly that her knuckles loudly cracked. She still couldn't believe she had mustered up the courage to confront Silas, even though she'd stumbled over half of her words. Still, telling him exactly what she thought of him was a small victory, even though they hadn't accomplished anything during their brief discussion.

Maybe agreeing to wait for Silas here in the gazebo was a bad idea, Leah thought, nearly tripping over her shoelaces that had become untied as a result of her hurried pacing. If they were alone, Silas might use her anxiety to his advantage, manipulating the conversation to get what he wanted. She couldn't let that happen. Maybe if she stood her ground,

Silas would change his mind about bringing his customers to her home. And if not, she was determined to make it clear that she wouldn't allow herself to be pushed around ever again.

"Sorry to keep you waiting," Silas apologized as he stepped into the gazebo. "I didn't want my customers to think I was ignoring them."

Leah spun around to face him so quickly that she nearly became dizzy. She hadn't heard him approaching the gazebo and disliked being caught off guard.

"Th-that's f-fine," she stammered, feeling her hands begin to shake once more. She balled her fingers into fists, trying to hide her nervousness. She wouldn't give Silas another reason to think she was weak.

Silas smiled awkwardly as he took a seat on the gazebo's bench. "Sure is *schee* weather we are having. Perfect for the start of the harvest, and the leaves will start changing color within the next few weeks. Fall is my favorite time of *yaahr*."

Leah scoffed, annoyed with his attempt to make small talk. Was he so thick that he thought this was a normal conversation? "I'm not here to t-talk about how n-nice the w-weather is."

Silas shrugged dramatically. "Just being

friendly," he said with hints of frustration and disappointment in his voice. He glanced away, though Leah wondered if it was to hide rolling eyes.

"W-we aren't f-friends." Leah's words were sharp, even to her own ears.

"Okay, let's get right to the point then." He motioned for Leah to sit beside him, but she shook her head. He shrugged again as he went on. "How do you feel about me bringing buggy rides to Leah's Countryside Cupboard? Do you think we can work together? It will benefit both of our businesses if my customers come to your roadside stand."

Leah crossed her slender arms over her chest. "M-maybe I w-would've been more agreeable to it if y-you came to me with this idea instead of only t-talking to my *daed*. You w-were s-sneaky about it." Even though it was a mild early-autumn day, she felt the boiling heat of embarrassment creeping up her neck, like a newly acquired sunburn. Silas probably thought her stutter was front and center, not the message that she was trying to convey.

"I'm awful sorry about that. To be honest, I did plan on speaking with you sooner, but I was worried that…well, I mean…since we haven't always been the best of friends…"

"And going behind my b-back was s-supposed to make me f-feel better about it?" Leah snapped back, interrupting his explanation. "Am I s-supposed to forget how you t-treated me for all those y-years?"

Silas let out an exasperated groan. "Look, I know you don't like me, and you probably never will, but I still think we can learn to work together." He turned and waved at Ivan and the group of tourists as the buggy passed by the gazebo. Once the horse and buggy had gone, he stood and walked toward her with a pleading expression. "I'm sorry for how I acted when I was a *bu*, but I've grown up. Please, Leah, just give me one chance to prove that to you." He extended his open hand to her, obviously hoping to shake on the proposed agreement to put their past behind them.

Leah's eyes narrowed again as she considered what Silas had said. It was true, she would never have any sort of fondness for him. Even though she was upset enough to have smoke pouring out of her ears, she hesitated, recalling the conversation she'd had with her father after yesterday's supper. If the Lord can forgive him, isn't it our duty to forgive Silas as well? Her father's question shook Leah to her core. Silas's childhood harassment caused her to develop an anxious outlook on life, worsening her stutter and stealing her inner peace.

She could never forgive him for that, but she could choose to treat him kindly.

"F-fine. You can bring t-tourists to our farm and the r-roadside stand." She looked down at his still-extended hand but refused to accept it. "I—I—I won't stand for any f-funny business," she firmly declared, pointing an accusing finger at him. Before Silas could reply, she brushed passed him and hurried out of the gazebo, glad to have gotten the last word.

Silas planted himself on the couch in the sitting room after supper that night, holding a notebook and pen. He intended to make a list of special chores that needed to be done for his business in the upcoming weeks, but he had difficulty concentrating on the task at hand. It wasn't the gentle hissing of the three gas lamps that distracted him, nor was it the quiet chatter of his parents, Paul and Barbara. The pair sat side by side on the loveseat, assembling a one-thousand-piece puzzle that they had been working on for the past few days.

Silas considered accepting their earlier invitation to work on the puzzle, but decided against it, knowing he would not be able to focus. The memory of Leah scolding him earlier that day remained at the front of his mind. It was hard to believe that timid, soft-spoken

Leah had raised her voice at him. Even more shocking, she'd agreed to give him a chance and allow him to bring tourists to her family's farm. Silas had gotten what he wanted by receiving Leah's permission, but he didn't feel as victorious as he thought he would.

"Penny for your thoughts, *sohn*," his father said without looking up from the puzzle pieces he was studying.

"Huh?" Silas had been staring at his blank notebook, lost in thought until his father addressed him.

His mother raised her head and grinned. "You've been quiet today." She gazed at him over her glasses that rested on the end of her nose. "I wonder if your quiet spell has anything to do with Leah Fisher. I saw you two talking in the gazebo this morning when I was hanging the wash on the clothesline."

"*Jah*, Leah was here earlier." Silas drummed his pen on the notebook, the fast-tapping sounds matching his accelerated heart rate. "I've been thinking about that conversation all day," he added grimly, talking to himself more than anyone else.

His parents exchanged curious glances. "Have you and Leah started courting?" his father asked, leaning forward in his chair.

A glint of hope sparkled in his mother's

light blue eyes as an expectant smile crossed her lips.

"*Ach, Daed*, of course not," Silas replied defensively, shocked that his father would even consider that to be a possibility. "We'll never go courting, and we probably won't ever see eye to eye, for that matter."

"Why not?" His mother asked, fidgeting with several glossy puzzle pieces. "Leah's a sweet *maedel*. I figured she'd have several young men hoping to win her attention."

Silas stifled a sigh. "I'm sure that's true, but she wants nothing to do with me." An uncomfortable silence passed through the tidy, spacious room. "You know how I was when I was a *bu* before I joined the church. I wasn't always...pleasant with her."

"*Ach*, Silas!"

His mother's shrill reaction and his father's deepening wrinkles let Silas know that they fully understood his explanation. Clearly, they were troubled when remembering the havoc he had caused during his youth, especially the mean streak he desperately wished to forget.

"*Vell*, you and Leah are both grown. The past can be put behind you," his father said, breaking the short silence. "No need to fuss over what can't be undone."

"I hope so," Silas replied. "Remember how I

mentioned that I wanted to expand my buggy rides and offer the option to tour an Amish farm?"

His parents both nodded.

"I decided the Fisher farm was the perfect place to take customers since it's not too far away and there's the bonus of Leah's roadside stand." He felt antsy and stood to relieve some restlessness. "Long story short, I asked Ezra Fisher for his permission to bring buggy rides to their farm, but I didn't say anything to Leah. That's why she was here today."

"So, you worked things out with her?" his father asked as he returned his gaze to the puzzle.

"Not exactly," Silas admitted hesitantly, making his way toward the windows. It was nearly dark outside, so he reached to pull down the dark green shades. "She did agree to let me bring folks to her business, but our conversation didn't go as well as I'd hoped."

"I see." His father gave his beard a few tugs, a familiar habit. "The best thing you can do is pray. Have faith that *Gott* will work things out between you."

"*Jah*, that's a *gut* idea," Silas agreed as he returned to his spot on the sofa, knowing that prayer might be the only thing that could help him.

"Hmm, I wonder…"

"What's that, *Mamm*?" Silas asked, wondering if his mother had been talking to herself.

"Remember that family over in Quarryville whose buggy was hit by a drunk driver? There's going to be a benefit auction tomorrow at the Esh farm to raise money for them," she replied, finally placing the puzzle piece that she'd been holding for several minutes.

Silas had nearly forgotten about tomorrow's benefit auction. Normally he'd anticipate the upcoming community event, but it had been pushed to the back of his mind ever since his confrontation with Leah.

"I ran into Fern Lapp a few days ago at King's Dry Goods and she told me that she and Leah will be sharing a booth at the auction," his mother went on. "Maybe you can stop by their booth and visit with Leah. Say something *siess* to her and maybe buy one of her baked goods." A motherly smile lit her face like the glow of a candle. "That will show her that you're making an effort to be on better terms. It's *gut* and very important to pray, but you also need to move your feet so *Gott* can direct your steps."

Knowing that his mother's words of wisdom were true, Silas came to a decision. He was planning on going to the auction anyway, hoping to get a good deal on a new buggy for his business. While he was there, he would stop by Leah's booth. He would just have to keep trying to smooth things over with her, though winning Leah over would be more difficult than trying to plow a frozen field in the middle of a January blizzard.

Chapter Four

When Saturday morning arrived, a layer of fog blanketed the village of Bird-in-Hand. By eight o'clock most of the fog had been burned off by the sun. Though the fog had disappeared, the previous evening's chill still lingered. Earthy scents of freshly harvested fields along with the nippy morning air refreshed Leah's senses as she arrived at the Esh farm, which was peacefully tucked away on Beechdale Road.

As she pulled her spring wagon into the Esh's gravel driveway, several of the young Esh boys greeted her enthusiastically. With bare feet and freckled faces, the boys directed Leah to guide her horse to a field that had been chosen as the designated parking lot. Half of the expansive field was reserved for *Englisch* vendors and guests, and a handful of automobiles were already parked there. Several dozen Amish buggies and wagons were already neatly lined up on the other half of the field. Twins Mervin and Micah Esh took great pride in showing Leah where she could bring her rig to a halt, while older brother Ben tended to Leah's horse. Before Leah could climb down from the wagon, Ben used a white grease crayon to mark the number twenty-seven on her horse's flank. Then he wrote the number on a slip of paper and handed it to Leah.

"Your number is *zwansich-siwwe*," Ben said, smiling up at her. "When you're ready to leave, just tell me what number your *gaul* is and I'll run and fetch him. I'll get him unhitched and take him to the pasture for you now."

"Are you gonna sell something or are you here to shop?" This question came from Mervin, the smallest of the boys. "We gotta make sure to raise lots of money for the *familye* who needs our help."

"I'm here to sell some b-baked goods, but I'll be sure to do some sh-shopping as well." Leah grinned at each of the industrious young men.

"My *brieder* will help you carry your things to the auction while I get your *gaul* taken care of," Ben declared matter-of-factly. "Holler for one of us if you need anything."

Leah chuckled and thanked all of the Esh boys for their help. She walked to the back of the wagon and undid the latch so that she and the twins could unload her baked goods. As soon as the small door on the back of the wagon fell open, Willow's head popped up from behind one of the crates.

"You brought your *hund* with you," Mervin gasped, staring wide-eyed at the Dalmatian as she jumped down from the carriage and circled around the group.

Leah held back a giggle. Willow had jumped in the wagon as she had been loading it, and even after some gentle coaxing, the dog refused to get out. She didn't have the heart to pull the faithful hound out and decided to allow Willow to come along.

"Never heard of a *hund* coming to an auction before," Micah declared, scratching the agreeable animal behind her ears.

"Really? Aren't d-dogs allowed here?" Leah asked, pretending to fret for the children's entertainment.

"*Ach,* of course! We have two *hund* of our own," Ben called as he led Leah's horse toward the pasture. "Maybe they'll become friends!"

Leah smiled at the idea of Willow becoming friends with the two Esh dogs as she reached for some of the crates in the back of her wagon.

After handing one to each of the twins she stacked the last two containers and lifted the bottom crate. She headed toward the auction grounds with Mervin, Micah and Willow following close behind.

When she reached the rolling pasture where the event was being held, Leah was surprised to see even more activity than she'd expected. The event wouldn't officially start for another half hour, but there were plenty of people already milling around. The scent of trampled, dew-covered grass mixed with the aroma of freshly brewed coffee from one of the vendor's stands. It was going to be a good day, and Leah was glad that Fern had invited her to share a booth.

It took Leah a short time to locate Fern, who stood behind three long folding tables arranged in the shape of a horseshoe. One full table and a half of another were loaded with Fern's crafts, which were arranged by color. The visually pleasing display included quilted tote bags and purses, throw pillows, lap blankets and potholders. Leah knew that the empty places on the tables were for her to fill with her baked goods, and she hoped she'd brought enough bread and pastries to fill her share of the space.

"Looks like you've got yourself three little

helpers," Fern said, grinning and placing her hands on her hips as the group approached the table.

"Only two helpers," Micah corrected Fern as he placed his crate on the table.

Fern pointed at Willow who promptly sniffed out a spot under one of the tables and plopped down to rest. "Maybe so, but Willow thinks she's helping."

Everyone laughed at Fern's observation. Leah thanked the Esh boys for their help and handed them three whoopie pies.

"Give that last one to B-Ben," she directed the boys before they scurried back to the make-shift parking lot. Then she unloaded baked goods and with the help of Fern's keen eye, the display of treats quickly covered the empty space on the tables.

"These all look downright tasty," Fern complimented Leah as both women took a seat in the folding chairs that Fern had brought along. "How did you manage to bake so much? Did you clear out your entire stock from the roadside stand to sell here today?"

Leah rubbed the back of her neck. "S-somewhat. I didn't want to leave my shop without any baked goods, so I never went to b-bed last night and s-stayed up baking instead."

Fern's green eyes grew wide as buggy wheels. "You must be exhausted."

Leah shook her head. "I was tired, but the c-cool morning air w-woke me up." A noisy yawn snuck up on her that she struggled to hide. The two friends stared at each other for a moment before laughing at Leah's predicament.

What would she do without Fern's loyal companionship? As a child, when her stutter was at its worst and her confidence was at its lowest, Leah had been detrimentally timid when she first started attending the one-room schoolhouse. That was until she met spunky Fern Lapp, the tall, red-haired second-grader who had gently coaxed her out of her shell.

A steady flow of customers visited Fern and Leah's booth over the next several hours. Just as soon as one customer paid for their items and walked away, two more customers approached. Leah was thankful for the business, knowing that all the profits made today were going directly to an Amish family whose buggy had been hit by a drunk driver and now found themselves with hefty hospital bills and the need to purchase a new buggy. The strong sense of community was something that Leah treasured about being Amish, and she was glad to be part of such a caring church family.

Just after noon, Leah turned away from the table and took a few sips from her water bottle. She hadn't found time for a break since the auction opened and she was feeling warm and parched. As she finished the last bit of water left in the bottle, she felt Fern tug on her hand.

"Someone just called your name," Fern said, pointing toward the crowd.

Leah turned and felt her stomach drop as Silas Riehl smiled and waved from about a dozen yards away.

"J-just perfect," Leah grumbled, feeling her chest tighten. "I was having a *w-wunderbaar* day, and here comes S-Silas to ruin it." She bit her tongue to stop herself from saying something she might regret. She felt like a tea kettle that was about to boil. Today's auction and companionship with Fern had been enough to make her forget her recent interaction with Silas and her hesitant agreement to partner their businesses. Now here he was again, coming to ruin her peace. It seemed like he was a pesky horsefly that refused to be shooed away.

"How could Silas ruin your day?" Fern asked as she began to rearrange some items to fill the empty table space.

Silas was approaching quickly, and Leah knew she didn't have time to discuss this with Fern. "We're about to f-find out."

* * *

Silas's stomach was starting to rumble but he didn't immediately notice his hunger pains. He was having such an enjoyable and successful day at the auction that it was hard for him to think of anything else. He'd bid on and won a gently used wagon, which he planned on converting into an additional carriage for his business. With October just around the corner and the addition of Amish farm tours, Silas expected his business to be busier than ever before, so expanding his fleet of carriages made sense.

After writing a check for his new investment, Silas wandered around the auction grounds to see what else might suit his fancy. He sampled several of the flavored teas and lemonades that one vendor offered but then decided he needed something more substantial. While scanning for vendors who were selling food items, he spotted Leah Fisher and Fern Lapp tending one of the many booths. Knowing that Leah would likely be selling some of her delicious pastries, he made his way toward their booth.

"*Guder mariye*, Leah," Silas called with a friendly wave and smile as he approached the booth. She must've not heard him since she didn't turn at the sound of her name. When

Fern said something to her, Leah spun around. Her lovely smile immediately turned upside down and her shoulders quickly rose and fell, like she'd heaved a great sigh.

Great, I haven't more than greeted her and she's already scowling at me.

Now that he'd been coldly acknowledged, Silas considered just passing by instead of having a clearly unwanted conversation. He could always go get a hot lunch from one of the many food trucks that were parked on the other side of the auction grounds. He slowed his pace as he considered this option, but then his mother's encouraging words came to mind. If he was ever to gain Leah's trust, he'd need to keep showing her that he was no longer the bully that he had once been.

"Guder mariye," Silas repeated his greeting as he stepped up to the booth. "Perfect day for the auction, *jah*?"

"For sure and for certain," Fern replied with a welcoming smile. She glanced at Leah quickly, her smile fading when she noticed her friend's sour expression. "Have you had a chance to bid on or buy anything today?" she asked, turning her attention back to him.

Silas explained that he'd bid on and won a used wagon that was almost like new. "But now I'm in search of something to eat, and everyone knows that Leah makes the best goodies." He gave his stomach a few pats, already imagining the flavorful treat he would soon have.

Leah's face flamed at the mention of her name. Maybe she was surprised by the compliment or perhaps she was becoming more agitated. "I'm afraid the s-selection I have has been p-picked over by the crowds we had earlier, and th-there's not much left."

"That's *oll recht.* My *mamm* didn't raise a picky eater," Silas replied, rubbing his hands together. He hoped his cheerful demeanor would win her over, but Leah's stern expression didn't change. Doing his best not to let her mood affect him, he quickly chose a package of a half dozen pumpkin cookies and a banana muffin, then handed them to Leah. "These look *appenditlich.*"

Leah held the cookies and muffin while Silas reached for his wallet. He pulled out a twenty-dollar bill and handed it to her. She accepted his payment and reached into her money pouch to prepare his change, but he stopped her. "No need for that."

Leah's eyebrows arched in confusion. "I owe you ch-change."

Silas shook his head. "*Nee*, you don't. Today's purpose is to raise funds for a good cause."

Leah hesitated for a moment, frozen like a

statue. She studied him intently as if she wasn't sure how to respond. Finally, she handed Silas the cookies and muffin, then placed his money in her pouch. *"D-denki."*

Pleased that Leah hadn't fought him on the matter, Silas tore open the muffin's plastic wrapping and took a bite. "This is *wunderbaar gut*, Leah. You're a talented baker!"

Once again Leah's face turned beet red. *"D-d-denki."* Silas thought he saw the corners of her mouth turning slightly upward, but her lips quickly dropped. The hint of a smile must have just been a nervous twitch.

"We're about to close our booth for a half hour to have ourselves a picnic lunch," Fern spoke up. "Would you like to join us?"

Leah shot Fern a horrified look.

"That sounds nice," he responded, "but I've got to head back to work soon. My business is open today and I need to check on my employees." He felt something cool and moist touch his hand. He glanced down to see a friendly Dalmatian sniffing his palm. He squatted down to pet the dog as she wagged her tail. "Nice *hund*! Is she yours, Leah?"

"Jah," came Leah's blunt reply, nearly as sharp as a paring knife.

"What's her name?"

"W-Willow," Leah answered sharply. She

snapped her fingers, which brought the dog back to her side.

Silas was surprised that she called Willow back. Did she not trust him to pet the animal? He anxiously adjusted his straw hat, worrying that anything he said or did might cause Leah to change her mind about allowing his buggy rides to visit her home.

He cleared his throat. "I just stopped to buy a snack and say hello. I guess I'll see you at church tomorrow and then again next Saturday."

"*Jah.*"

Realizing that he wasn't going to get much more out of Leah, Silas decided it was time to leave. He smiled and bid farewell to the women.

As he took another bite of the muffin, he couldn't help but think about the lucky fellow who would one day marry Leah. *Whomever that man might be, he will certainly never go hungry*, Silas thought as he finished the muffin. Leah was attractive and also a talented baker and smart businesswoman. He thought he would possibly be interested in courting her someday if she ever warmed up to him. Silas scoffed at that idea. The most he could hope for was to earn her friendship, and that would certainly be enough.

Chapter Five

❧

"You look upset," Fern said to Leah as they sat down at one of the picnic tables that the Esh family had provided for the vendors and auction-goers.

Leah reached into her lunch box and withdrew her sandwich, though she was no longer in the mood for it. Silas's sudden appearance had not only ruined her appetite but had also ruined her previously carefree day.

"I don't w-want to talk about it," she replied honestly, hoping that Fern would change the topic of their conversation.

Fern shot Leah a pointed look that quickly softened. "As your best friend, I can't accept that answer." She paused for a moment. "What did Silas mean when he said he would see you next Saturday?"

Leah bit her tongue to try to keep from grinning. There was something about Fern's direct yet gentle nature that she found reassuring. If there was anyone she could confide in, it was Fern.

"I'm upset that S-Silas wants to bring his buggy ride c-customers to our farm and my shop." She stared down at her untouched sandwich and folded her shaking hands. "He stopped by earlier this w-week and bought a whoopie pie but said n-nothing about b-bringing folks to our farm. He b-brought up his idea to my *daed*, but not to m-me."

Fern reached into her lunch bag, pulled out a large green apple, and took a bite of the fruit. "From what he said earlier, it sounded like you've already agreed to receive his buggy rides at your place."

Leah picked up her sandwich and held it without taking a bite. "*Jah*, but he didn't talk to me about the p-plan until I c-confronted him." She forced herself to take a bite of her sandwich, though her sullen mood made the light meal seem tasteless. After brushing some crumbs from her face, she shared the root of what was bothering her. "It feels s-sneaky since he w-went behind my back."

Fern nodded sympathetically. "I can see why that would bother you, but I don't think it's anything to be angry about."

"Who's angry?" The friends looked up to see Martha, one of Leah's elder, married sisters. She carried her fourteen-month-old son, Toby, in one arm and the handle of a small picnic basket in the other. Both Leah and Fern welcomed Martha and Toby to the table. Leah eagerly took her nephew from his mother's arms so Martha would be free to eat her lunch.

"I'm g-glad to see you two," Leah greeted them enthusiastically. She gently kissed the top of Toby's head and bounced the happy child on her knee. She was thankful for their arrival since it provided a desperately needed interruption.

Martha smiled as she reached into her picnic basket and withdrew a small jar of homemade applesauce and a disposable spoon. She handed the items to Leah. "I'm glad to see you as well. Now I'll be able to hear about what's making you angry."

Leah groaned inwardly. As she slowly fed Toby, who playfully smacked his lips after each spoonful of applesauce, she told Martha about Silas's plan to bring tourists from his buggy ride business to their father's farm and her roadside stand. She also shared the tale of how Silas had avoided telling her about his plans.

"It makes me sick to my s-stomach to think

that I'll have to s-see him every day," Leah confessed, using a napkin to wipe Toby's messy face. The little boy squirmed at first, but once the cleanup was over, he snuggled against Leah's chest. She cuddled the toddler close to her heart, relishing the comfort that he unknowingly provided.

"Hold on," Fern spoke up after she took the last bite of her apple. "I think it's possible that Silas feels bad about how he pestered you when we were *kinner.* That's probably why he put off discussing his plans with you."

Leah shrugged, somewhat perturbed that her closest friend was speaking in Silas's defense. What Fern said was true, though. Her conscious pricked at her the way a quilting needle could stab at a thimble-free thumb.

Martha gazed at Leah with compassion. "I can recall how Silas treated you when you were younger, and I can see how his unkind words affected your confidence throughout the years. It was a cruel thing for him to do, but that was so long ago."

Fern bobbed her head in agreement. "Silas had no right to tease about something that you have no control over. On the bright side, your speech has improved so much! You're a strong woman now."

"That's right," Martha agreed fervently.

"You also can't forget how much Silas has matured since then. He's not that little trouble-maker anymore. Since he repented from the things of this world and joined the church, he's been respectable and quite friendly."

"I know you're r-right," Leah muttered so quietly that she wasn't sure if Martha and Fern heard what she said. Fighting off tears, Leah glanced down at the bundle in her arms. With his head pressed against her chest, little Toby had fallen asleep in Leah's embrace. She gently rocked the sweet child, hoping he'd never face such heartache. "I suppose I'm just b-bitter."

Fern wrapped her arm around Leah. "Bitterness has a way of hurting the person who holds it."

"You've got such a sweet spirit, Leah. I don't think you have it in you to be bitter for the rest of your life, especially over a childhood bully," Martha added.

Martha's tender words tugged at Leah's heart. She mustered a small, genuine grin, consoled by the words of these two special ladies.

"Besides," Martha went on as she pulled a turkey wrap out of her basket, "you don't have to like Silas. You just need to be kind to him. That'll make it easier for both of you since you'll be seeing each other more often."

"Plus, this opportunity might be a blessing

in disguise," Fern observed as she tossed her apple core into the nearby waste bin. "Silas bringing wagonloads of folks to Leah's Countryside Cupboard will mean even more business for you and your family."

"I h-hope so," Leah agreed hesitantly. As Fern and Martha chatted about the auction and the lovely weather, Leah stroked Toby's blond hair. She rested her cheek gingerly atop the child's shiny locks, wondering if she would be able to rouse the same positive outlook that Fern and Martha shared. At that moment, her favorite scripture verse came to mind. *With* Gott *all things are possible*, Leah reminded herself, *even when it comes to getting along with Silas Riehl.*

After making one last sweep through the vendors to make sure he hadn't overlooked a bargain or treasure, Silas decided to leave the auction. He'd been having a decent day, but the earlier interaction he'd had with Leah weighed heavily on his mind. Although their interaction could have gone worse, there was still a great deal of tension between them, and Silas was eager to do whatever he could to break it.

As he made his way through the crowded auction grounds, he noticed a cluster of picnic tables situated a small distance from the vendors' booths. Leah sat at one of the tables with her sister Martha and Fern Lapp.

Silas glanced down at the package of pumpkin cookies in his hand, then thought about the delicious muffin he'd also purchased from Leah.

Should I go over there and tell her how much I enjoyed her baking? Maybe a genuine compliment would help her to see that I'm not such a bad guy, he thought.

Silas stood in place as he mulled the idea over. When he spotted the disgruntled look on Leah's face and the concerned expressions that Martha and Fern were wearing, he decided against approaching them. Leah was probably venting to them about her reluctant agreement to partner their businesses, and it would be awkward, if not borderline impolite, to intrude on that conversation.

Oh well, Silas thought as he made his way to the parking area to find his waiting buggy. *I'll just have to keep my eyes open for more opportunities to win Leah over.*

The biweekly church gathering was held at Martha's house the next morning, and Leah enjoyed every minute of worship and fellowship. The nearly three-hour service was held in the freshly cleaned barn where the congregation was seated on backless wooden benches. Men and older boys were seated on one side while women, girls and small children were seated on the other. The time was filled with the singing of hymns, scripture readings, silent prayers and various sermons that were preached by the church leaders. After the usual lengthy service, a light lunch was served to the churchgoers.

Martha was a smart hostess and served her church family their meals using disposable plates, cups and utensils. This left only a small amount of kitchen cleanup, and with the help of her younger sisters, Leah and Sarah, plus Fern Lapp, Martha's kitchen was quickly being whipped back into shape.

As she dried the serving platters that Martha had scrubbed clean, Leah had trouble keeping up with the lively conversation. Her mind continued to revisit the church service. She was in good spirits after spending time in prayer, spilling her heart to the Lord and asking for his intervention in her life. On top of that, she recalled a humorous moment that had occurred during the service. Henry Lapp, Fern's great-grandfather had fallen asleep and let out one loud snore. The elderly fellow had startled himself awake, causing a few muted chuckles from the congregation. It had been a wonderful Lord's Day, and Leah was glad to spend this time with her church family.

"I think that serving dish is dry now," Martha said as she used her elbow to tap Leah's side, stirring her sister out of her daydreaming.

Leah flinched and glanced at Martha who was letting the soapy water down the drain. Then she turned to Fern who stared curiously, waiting to take the dry platter from her.

"S-sorry," she apologized, shaking her head to clear her mind. She handed the dish to Fern and then draped the damp dishtowel over the sink faucet.

Fern placed the dish into its spot on the cupboard and then eyed Leah suspiciously. "You're quiet and smiley."

"*Jah*, what's on your mind?" Martha asked as she leaned against the kitchen counter.

"Th-thinking about the service, I g-guess," Leah answered truthfully. She held back a smile, mentally replaying Henry Lapp's loud snore.

Martha and Fern exchanged coy glances. "Never seen anyone smile so much after listening to a sermon about humility," Fern pointed out as she waltzed to one of the chairs at Martha's table. She dropped into the seat, put her elbows on the table, and cradled her cheeks in the palms of her hands. "What do you think, Martha?"

Martha, who was a bit more soft-spoken than Fern, clicked her tongue. "Can't say I ever brightened up like a full moon at such a serious topic."

Leah said nothing, not wanting to speak poorly of old Henry or embarrass Fern over her very elderly grandfather's actions. Perhaps they already knew what had her grinning and were also too polite to mention the incident.

"I thought the preaching went on longer than usual," Sarah announced as she stood from her spot on the floor and hopped into the chair next to Fern. "By the time the third sermon was over, my legs were asleep!"

The three women laughed at Sarah's innocent admission, and Leah was thankful for her younger sister's perfectly timed interruption. Still chuckling, Leah scooped up Toby, who had been crawling around the floor, and joined her little sister and Fern at the table. "I th-thought that might have happened s-since you were *rutsching* around more than T-Toby ever does."

The ladies chuckled again, and this time Sarah joined in the laughter. Toby must have wanted to be a part of the fun since he started to giggle too. His sweet childish squeals caused everyone to laugh even harder, and soon everyone was howling.

The screen door creaked open, and a gaggle of young men stepped inside. The group of fellows talked among themselves and surveyed the kitchen. Timothy, Martha's husband, and the only bearded man in the group moved forward. "Got anything we could munch on?"

Martha let out a playful scoff. "You just ate lunch. Are you telling me you're already *hungerich* again?"

Levi King, another one of the young fellows, gave his stomach several pats. "Why sure, we're growing *buwe*!" This comment caused everyone but Martha to chuckle.

Martha rolled her large chocolate eyes. "Well, you're certainly the largest *buwe* I've ever seen." The corners of her mouth turned upward, and she gave a playful wink.

When Timothy wandered toward the cabinets and opened one of the doors for a peek inside, Martha reached for the recently used dish towel that was drying and teasingly used it to slap her husband's hands away. "We just finished straightening up in here. There's some cheese and crackers on the table. Please help yourselves."

When the group of men shuffled toward the table, Leah stood and handed Toby to Fern.

She reached for the serving platter and held it out so each man could easily select the items he wanted. A small line quickly formed, restoring some order to Martha's tidy kitchen. As each man selected a few small cuts of cheese and a handful of crackers, they thanked Martha and exited the house just as quickly as they had entered.

In the sudden commotion, Leah hadn't noticed that Silas had entered the kitchen with the group. He stood quietly at the end of the line, patiently waiting for his turn to get a snack. He stepped up to her and gave her a half-hearted smile.

"Sorry that we interrupted your conversation," Silas apologized. "I guess we did barge in here like overgrown *buwe*."

"*Ach*, no bother at all." Martha shrugged as she waved the dish towel through the air. "Can I get you anything else? Some fruit? A glass of meadow tea?"

Before Silas could respond, Toby let out an ear-piercing scream, which caused everyone to flinch. Tears rolled down his chubby cheeks as he squirmed in Fern's arms like a caught fish.

"What's he hollering about?" Sarah asked as she covered her ears.

"He just ate so he's not *hungerich*," Martha stated, raising her voice to be heard above Toby's crying.

"M-maybe he needs his *windle* changed," Leah suggested, stepping toward Fern, and reaching for her nephew. "I c-can go check."

"Wait, maybe he wants this," Silas interjected as he picked up a teddy bear that was laying in the middle of the floor. He walked over to Leah and Toby and held out the toy. "Is this what you want, little guy? Were you missing your bear?"

Toby stopped wailing and rubbed away his tears with his pudgy fists. He shyly held out his hands for the bear.

Before Silas placed the toy in Toby's hands, he gently pressed the bear's snout against the boy's cheeks and made some kissing sounds. Toby perked up immediately and started to giggle.

Leah couldn't believe what she was witnessing. How had Silas known why Toby was so upset before any of the women did, including his mother? She knew Silas would never be cruel to such a little child, but it still stunned her to see him act in such a gentle manner. Was this new behavior, or was he putting on a show since he needed to get on her good side? Had she been purposely blinding herself to his positive attributes and didn't recognize the man he now was?

"How did you know that he wanted that raggedy old bear?" Martha asked, stepping toward Leah and Toby, then brushing the child's bowl-cut bangs out of his eyes.

Silas shrugged. "I don't know. Us men must all think alike, I guess."

His reply caused a chorus of chortles from everyone in the room, including Leah. She never thought she'd be near Silas and smile at the same time. First a wonderful church meeting, and then a positive moment with Silas; the Lord must have felt like blessing her twice that day.

Chapter Six

After the church service and the following light meal were concluded, most of the families in attendance decided to spend some additional time at the home of Timothy and Martha Stoltzfus. It was common in their church district for folks to linger and visit with their friends and neighbors well into the afternoon. Silas usually enjoyed catching up with his friends after the biweekly gatherings, but today he was eager to head home.

I probably wouldn't make good company anyway, Silas grumbled to himself as he scurried into the barn after making some necessary small talk with those who had stopped him to chat. Then he located his ebony-colored mare, Socks, and led the animal out of the barn while images of Leah paraded through his mind. He recalled glancing around the room during the church service, finding it hard not to take notice of Leah's lovely smile. She was a true beauty, but more importantly, she was a devout member of the church and had a gentle spirit about her. As he admired her, his mood suddenly plummeted. He could think nice things about Leah all day, but all the niceties in the world wouldn't soften her heart toward him.

As Silas worked to hitch Socks to his buggy, he heard light, hurried footsteps approaching over the silky grass. Thinking nothing of it, he stepped toward his buggy. Before he could climb into the rig, a gentle, stuttering female voice caught his attention.

"*Daed?* Is th-that you?"

Startled, Silas turned to see Leah. "Nope, just me," he replied with a half grin.

Leah's hand flew to her mouth as she realized her mistake. "S-sorry. Should've noticed that you w-weren't my *daed.*"

"Jah, since I don't have a beard." Silas rubbed his clean-shaven chin, which signaled to members of his community that he was unmarried. He offered her a leery smile, hoping that his statement of the obvious had been interpreted only as gentle teasing.

Surprisingly, Leah offered him a smile in return. "*Jah*, and no b-belly either," she pointed out as she gracefully tossed one of her *kapp*'s ribbons over her shoulder.

"I guess so." His grin widened as he enjoyed his very first private, cordial interaction with Leah. It felt almost like an answered prayer, seeing her smile at him as if they had always been on friendly terms. He decided not to say any more on that matter, not wanting to joke at her father's expense. "Anything I can help you with?"

Leah's smile twisted and faded. "My *m-mamm* has a headache and w-wants to go home. I was just t-trying to find my *daed* so we can leave."

"Sorry to hear that," Silas replied as concern etched across his face. "I'm heading out now, and I could give your *mamm* a ride home if you…if she would like."

Leah's hazel eyes blinked several times as if she was surprised by the offer. "*D-denki*, but *Daed* will want to be the one to see that *Mamm* g-gets home. He worries about her when she's f-feeling *grank*."

"I understand." Silas nodded, shifting his weight from one leg to the other. "I saw him chatting with Abner Ebersol on the porch swing right before I came out to get my horse, so he's probably still there. You know how Abner likes to gab."

Leah brightened again. *"D-denki."* She wrung her hands together as a few seconds of silence passed. She looked up at Silas as if she was unsure of how to excuse herself. She nodded slightly before brushing past him and heading toward the house.

Silas felt his heart rate rise as a sudden burst of confidence erupted in his spirit. Leah hadn't immediately walked away once she realized her mistake, and she even felt comfortable enough to participate in some banter. This was certainly promising, and far more than Silas had expected of his first interaction with Leah following their awkward conversation at the benefit auction.

"Leah," Silas called to her retreating form, deciding to take a risk before he lost his nerve.

When she stopped in her tracks and turned to face him with a curious expression on her pretty face, Silas nearly forgot what he was going to say.

He cleared his throat a few times before he spoke again. "If you were planning on staying here longer, I wouldn't mind... I mean... I could give you a ride home."

Leah glanced over his shoulder at his waiting horse and buggy. "Looks like you're r-ready to leave now."

Silas craned his neck to look at Socks, who

stomped her hoof against the ground. "*Jah*, but if you wanted to stay, I would stay with you."

Leah's lips parted as she stared at him with bewilderment.

Silas stumbled to explain himself. "I mean, I wouldn't mind waiting for you. That is… I'd be glad to give you a ride home if you wanted to visit with your friends or *schwester* some more." He let his gaze drop to the ground and shoved his hands into his pockets to keep from smacking himself in the face. *I just had to make that awkward, didn't I?*

Leah tilted her head to the side, almost as if she was considering the offer. After several painfully long seconds passed, her shoulders rose in a small shrug. "Th-that's *oll recht. Denki* for the offer, th-though." She quietly cleared her throat. "T-Toby seems to like you."

Silas couldn't help but smile. "*Denki*, I like him too. Ever since my *schwester* Barbie and her *mann* Jacob had *kinner*, I've had a special place in my heart for little ones." He stared at the ground, kicking at a weed near the toe of his boot. "When they were born, it gave me another reason to settle down and join the church. They need a respectable *onkel*, after all."

Leah grinned and nodded understandingly. "Toby is my only n-nephew, but he's v-very special to me." She dropped her gaze to the grass, which had lost a bit of its green vibrancy now that autumn was knocking on the door. "I better g-g-go find my *daed*. Have a *gut* d-day." She raised her hand in a small wave and then made a beeline toward her sister's house.

"*Jah*, you too." Silas beamed, thrilled to his core. Although their conversation had been short, it had been the best one they'd ever had. Maybe this pleasant interaction meant they were on their way to being on better terms, and perhaps they might even be friends one day. The most important thing was that Leah was learning to be comfortable around him. Since he would soon be seeing her daily, there was plenty of time for her to get to know the real Silas and forget the terror he had been as a boy.

After she changed into her long cotton nightgown, brushed her torso-length hair, and said her evening prayers, Leah pulled back the light summer quilt and crawled into bed. She sighed and closed her eyes, ready for a good night's sleep. It had been a pleasant, spiritually fulfilling day, except for the headache that her mother had suffered from for a few hours. Leah noticed that her anxiety had been at an unusual low, and she didn't take that for granted. She stretched and yawned contentedly, expecting to drift off to sleep in no time.

A few moments passed before her eyes snapped open. She clambered out of bed and rushed to the floral calendar that hung on her wall. Using the moonlight that spilled into her open window, she ran her finger over the calendar page to the date that she had marked with a small check. She cringed as her suspicion was confirmed. Tomorrow would be the first day that Silas would start bringing buggy rides to Leah's Countryside Cupboard.

The calm, carefree mood she'd enjoyed earlier immediately evaporated. The tranquility of her world was about to be disrupted, and the constant discomfort that she'd dealt with as a child was about to come charging back into her life like a bull that had escaped the barnyard. Her business, the thing she loved and found fulfillment in, would soon be plagued with constant uncertainty as she remained on edge, always looking over her shoulder whenever Silas was around.

That isn't fair, her conscience whispered, forcing her to confront her bias toward Silas. After all, he'd been cordial with her recently. Leah also caught a glimpse of his gentle side when he interacted with Toby earlier that day.

She groaned and dragged herself back to

bed. Every time she thought of Silas, she faced a whirlwind of emotions. There was mistrust and hurt, plus her own guilt for not being able, or willing, to put the past behind them.

She rolled onto her side and stared out the window, not caring that her feet were tangled in the bedsheets. The ebony night sky was crystal clear, and each star seemed within reach. As she gazed into the universe that the Almighty One had created, she sent up a heartfelt request.

Lord, please calm my anxious heart. Give me the strength to cope with the unwanted changes that are happening in my life.

"So, the Amish people don't use any power at all?"

While keeping both hands on the reins, Silas glanced at the tourist woman seated behind him in the carriage. "Not exactly," he answered politely. "Different church groups allow different power sources. Most of the Amish folks around here use gas to power their refrigerators, stoves, and similar things." He clicked his tongue and pulled the reins, signaling his two large draft horses to turn onto Stumptown Road. "Some Amish use solar power, batteries, and quite a few use a windmill to pump water into the house."

His customers, three older *Englisch* couples, began to chat among themselves about life without modern conveniences and the "quaint-ness" of the plain lifestyle. Silas returned his full attention to the road, trying to ignore his apprehension. This was the first group of tour-ists that he was bringing to the Fisher farm, and he was nervous about seeing Leah. He had no doubt that she would warmly welcome his guests, but he worried about how his presence would be received, even after their nice con-versation at the preaching service yesterday. For what felt like the umpteenth time, Silas regretted his boyhood actions as he listened to the rhythmic clip-clopping of the horses' hooves.

"Excuse me, sir?"

Silas snapped out of his daydreaming. He adjusted his position on the seat so he could look at his customers and also focus on the road with only slight head movements. *"Jah?"*

The same salt-and-pepper-haired tourist woman spoke up again. "I asked about the dif-ferent groups you mentioned. I always thought that all Amish people followed the same rules."

As the carriage neared the Fisher farm, Silas explained how different church districts held different ideas regarding clothing styles, re-strictions on modern conveniences, and other cultural things. The group of tourists asked several more questions as they snapped pictures of the farms, fields of Holstein cattle, and other horse-drawn vehicles that they passed by. Silas couldn't blame them since there was a lot to see, especially from a visitor's point of view. He also enjoyed traveling down Stumptown Road since it was scenic and generally quiet. The country road was even more peaceful than usual since it was still early morning. Truthfully, Silas was surprised to have customers as soon as his business opened at eight o'clock since people usually didn't start showing up until after nine.

I hope we're not too early, Silas thought, and felt worried as he guided the horses into the Fishers' driveway. As they neared the hitching rail beside Leah's Countryside Cupboard, he noticed the Closed sign hung on the tiny shop's door. He groaned inwardly, hoping their early arrival wouldn't give Leah another reason to hold a grudge.

"I'm going to hop out and tie the horses up, folks. Please stay seated until I come to the back of the carriage," he instructed his customers. "The shop isn't open yet, so I'll show you around the farm first."

After they had climbed down from the carriage, he led the tourists up the Fisher driveway and was promptly greeted by Willow. The excited pooch wagged her tail and greeted each person individually. The tourists were enamored with the dog and stopped to scratch her head.

The sound of a screen door squeaking open caused him to look up. There was Leah, looking flushed and perturbed. She hurried toward Silas and the group of tourists, balancing her nephew, Toby, on her hip and carrying a basket that was filled with muffins.

"I'm so sorry to k-keep you waiting." She smiled at the tourists. "W-welcome to our farm!" She extended her hand that held the basket. "I haven't had a ch-chance to open my shop yet, so p-please help yourself to a muffin while Silas takes you around the f-farm."

The group of *Englischers* thanked Leah for her hospitality as they each took a muffin from the basket.

"Folks, if you'd like to sit down with your snack, you can head over to the picnic tables that are behind the shop. Then we can carry on with our tour," Silas suggested as he motioned toward the roadside stand. The tourists agreed and ambled toward the tables as they unwrapped their muffins and discussed how beautiful the farm was.

Silas offered Leah an apologetic smile.

"Sorry to be so early. I didn't realize the stand wasn't open yet."

Leah frowned, though her mild scowl didn't make her any less lovely. "I d-don't open it until nine."

Silas bobbed his head, making a mental note. "Good to know for the future." To ease the tension, Silas focused on Toby. "Hello, young man." He reached for the toddler's chubby hand and gave it a shake. "Are you gonna help Leah in the shop today?" He spoke in Pennsylvania Dutch since Toby wouldn't learn English until he started attending school.

Leah's expression softened as she readjusted her hold on the boy. "I'm watching him for M-Martha while she goes to the d-dentist." Silas thought he noticed a hint of a smile as she glanced down at her nephew.

"I'm sure Toby will be a big help," Silas declared, gently tousling the boy's bowl-cut hair.

Toby giggled uncontrollably, then reached his little arms toward his head to smooth his hair.

Leah chuckled, then looked up at Silas, her full lips quickly falling back into their familiar stern expression. "I better go open the shop so the t-tourists can look around." Without waiting for a reply, Leah made a beeline toward the roadside stand.

Silas ambled back to his customers to see if they were ready to continue with their tour. Today hadn't gotten off to a great start, but things were slowly looking up.

Silas led the group to the enormous Fisher barn with Willow following their every move. They first passed by one of the meadows where the Fishers' two standard-bred buggy horses, four mules and a large herd of Holstein cattle were peacefully grazing. Silas led the curious tourists through the barn, pointing out the cattle stalls, milking equipment and the silage that the cattle ate. Moving toward the milk house, Silas showed the onlookers the tank where the milk was collected and then refrigerated in between weekly pickups that were made by truck. As they exited the barn, he pointed out the Fishers' gray buggy and stood back while the tourists snapped some photos.

"Leah's Countryside Cupboard should be open for business now," Silas said as they approached the shop. "Feel free to look around for as long as you'd like, and I'll meet you near the carriage when you're ready to go." He held the shop's door open for the tourists as they filed inside. Feeling a slight rumble in his stomach, he decided to see what kind of snacks Leah had for sale. He walked past a display of hand-sewn lap quilts, then around the shelves filled with homemade jams and jellies before he reached the baked goods. The small business seemed crowded, and Silas saw that he needed to wait his turn to choose something to nibble on. A small cluster of customers crowded around the display of cookies, muffins, whoopie pies, turnovers and bread, proving the popularity of Leah's baking skills.

After choosing a mint chocolate whoopie pie, Silas headed toward the counter where the battery-powered cash register was located. He was surprised to see Leah's younger sister, Sarah, manning the cashier's post.

Placing the pastry on the counter, he grinned at the girl and greeted her. "Awful busy this morning, *jah*?"

Sarah nodded enthusiastically, a smile warming her freckled cheeks. "Sure is! A small tour bus arrived shortly after your group did. *Daed* said I could stay home from *schul* today to help Leah."

Silas's mouth dropped open. "I didn't even notice the bus," he admitted. A twinge of guilt threatened to gnaw at him. Was it his fault that Sarah was missing school? Surely, the money that his tourists spent would supplement the Fishers' income, but he sincerely hoped that the added hecticness wasn't putting a strain on Leah or any of her family members. He glanced over his shoulder to see Leah standing next to a customer, seemingly answering the woman's questions about the lap quilts. She seemed flushed, but nevertheless, her smile lit up the entire room.

Silas cleared his throat, forcing himself to refocus his attention on his interaction with Sarah. "Do you mind skipping *schul* today?"

Sarah leaned over the counter as if she was about to whisper a secret. "Not even a little bit."

Silas chuckled then reached into his pocket for his wallet.

"There's no charge for this," Sarah interrupted him, pushing the whoopie pie across the counter. "Leah said that you're *wilkumme* to have whatever goodies you like when you stop by with a load of tourists."

Silas couldn't hide his growing smile. "That's very kind of her," he replied, still fishing in his pocket for his wallet. Once he had a hold of it, he opened the wallet and pulled out a few dollars. "Consider this a tip for your friendly service." Sarah accepted the money and thanked Silas before wishing him a good day.

Silas felt an added spring in his step as he headed for the exit. At some point today, Leah must have experienced some pleasant thoughts about him. Why else would she tell Sarah to make sure he received a treat, free of charge? Of course, that might be her way of thanking him for the added business. He shook his head to stop himself from overthinking it. His customers were enjoying their tour and Leah had only briefly scowled at him. This was turning out to be a nice day.

As Silas reached the door, he felt something brush past him. He looked down and chuckled when he saw Toby toddling around as he munched on a giant cookie. He looked adorable in his little green shirt, suspenders and black trousers.

The little fellow looked up at Silas and held up his cookie for his inspection. *"Gut,"* Toby said before taking another bite of the cookie.

"Jah, it does look *gut,"* Silas replied, though Toby was already padding away to show someone else his treasure. The sociable child approached one of his customers and tugged on the hem of her knee-length denim skirt.

The middle-aged woman gasped and then immediately beamed down at the boy.

"David," the woman gushed, tapping her husband on the shoulder, "have you ever seen such a sweet face?"

Toby held the cookie up in the air so the woman could get a good look at it before quickly pulling it away to take another baby-sized bite.

"I just have to get his picture!"

Silas instinctively stepped forward to politely remind the tourist that Amish people do not pose for photographs, but it was too late.

The woman quickly whipped a cell phone out of her purse, pointed it at Toby, and said, "Say cheese!"

Great, I hope Leah didn't see that, Silas thought as he started to panic, wishing with all of his might that nothing would ruin the small but significant headway he'd recently made with her.

Chapter Seven

"And all of these throw quilts are hand-stitched?"

"That's r-right," Leah said, bobbing her head as she answered the *Englisch* customer's question. "My friend Fern s-sewed each one by hand."

"They're so lovely that I simply have to get one," the young lady replied. She placed her hands on her small waist as she studied the display of blankets. "One of these would make a nice present for my mom's birthday. The only problem is that I can't seem to choose one."

Leah held in a sigh that ached to be released. Since the moment she awoke, the morning had been zooming by and she felt like she didn't have a moment to catch her breath. First, Martha had dropped off Toby so she could go to her dental appointment. Leah wasn't sure if he had eaten breakfast, so she'd given him a small bowl of oatmeal, which he promptly threw on the floor, making a mess and shattering the bowl. She had just cleaned up after that ordeal when she heard a buggy with a double team pull into the driveway. She knew without looking that Silas had arrived with his first group of visitors. She was already running late in preparing the shop for opening, and customers had arrived nearly a half hour early. By the time she opened the roadside stand, several cars and a small tour bus had filled up all the spots in the parking lot. Assisting her guests and keeping a close eye on Toby had become nearly impossible to do alone, so her father had mercifully allowed Sarah to skip one day of school so that she could lend a hand in the shop.

"Which one would you choose?" the young woman asked Leah, recapturing her attention.

Leah dug deep into the pile of neatly folded lap quilts until she found a white and lavender one. "I think this one is the n-nicest." She shook the folds out of the blanket and held it up for the woman's inspection. "It's somewhat l-larger than the others, but still the same p-price."

The woman's face lit up. "I'll take it!"

Leah grinned, pleased that her customer

was excited by her purchase. "Let me j-just fold this up for you." As she folded the throw and smoothed out the wrinkles, she heard an older woman's voice gushing over how cute something was. She glanced over her shoulder to see an *Englisch* woman beaming down at Toby. It warmed Leah's heart to know that others thought her nephew was just as precious as she did.

She handed the quilt to the customer she was assisting and asked her if she needed anything else.

As the young lady was speaking, Leah noticed a flash out of the corner of her eye. She spun around to see the middle-aged woman using a cell phone to snap photos of Toby.

That's one of the tourists Silas brought here, Leah grumbled inwardly, irritated by the woman's disrespectful actions. "Excuse m-me," she huffed as she marched toward the photographer, squeezing her way through the crowded aisle.

Just as she was about to reach the woman, Silas approached the customer from the other side.

"Pardon me, ma'am. Please don't photograph this young man or any of the other Amish people you'll encounter during your visit."

Leah stopped in her tracks, genuinely surprised that Silas intervened. She scooped Toby into her arms, then stepped back to watch the encounter, hoping that Silas wouldn't make too big of a scene.

The woman's smile faded as her cheeks flushed. "Did I do something wrong?"

An understanding smile crossed Silas's face. "We don't pose for photos since the Bible instructs us not to make any graven images."

The woman's hand flew to her mouth. "I'm so sorry! I know you folks don't like to have your picture taken, but I assumed the boy wouldn't mind." The woman's eyes darted between Leah and Silas. "I apologize!"

Silas put his hand up to stop the woman's frenzied expression of remorse. "Don't be sorry, it was just a misunderstanding. Enjoy the rest of your visit, and I'll meet you and everyone else outside in a few minutes."

The woman sheepishly apologized once more before continuing her shopping. Silas turned to face Leah and Toby, smiling sympathetically. "Can I talk to you outside for a moment?" he asked her.

Leah, still holding Toby as he finished his cookie, nodded, and then stomped outside.

Fuming, she hurried toward Silas's waiting team of draft horses. The hitching rail was at the farthest edge of the small parking lot, which was a good place to confront Silas about this situation. Leah herself had been the subject of some unwanted photos taken by tourists who didn't know about or had little respect for her culture, and she knew there was little that could be done to stop folks from occasionally snapping photos.

If Silas had taken the time to tell his guests not to take photos of them, Toby's image wouldn't exist in that woman's phone! Leah was under the impression that he had assured her *daed* that he and his customers would be respectful when visiting their farm. She seethed, growing madder than a hornet. When she reached the large horses, she stopped in her tracks and spun around to face her adversary.

Silas stood back, several feet away from Leah and Toby, as if to give her the space she needed. "I'm awful sorry about that." He rocked on his heels. "I should have told my customers not to take pictures of any of the Amish folks they might encounter while visiting your home."

"*Jah*, you sh-should h-have," Leah snapped, tightening her hold on Toby since he had started to squirm. She clung to the child as if he was a safety blanket that provided her the courage she desperately needed to give Silas a piece of her mind. "You sh-should've come up with a p-plan before you s-started b-bringing folks here!" She felt irritation bubbling in her chest. Her emotional state added fuel to her stutter, and the fact that she couldn't clearly communicate her frustration was even more upsetting. "You m-may have b-been able to push me around in the p-past, but you c-can't anymore!"

Silas's face clouded over. "I never want you to think that I'm pushing you around."

Sensing Leah's agitation, Toby wiggled harder and started to pout.

Leah gingerly set the boy on his feet in hopes that he would calm down. Her eyebrows rose as the child wobbled toward Silas, reaching his arms in the air. Silas bent down and playfully snatched the boy from the ground, and then gave him a few bounces. Toby giggled and wrapped his arms around Silas's neck in a sweet embrace.

Silas turned his attention back to Leah. "You're right. I should've set a few ground rules. I'm sorry."

Leah's mouth fell open and she stared at Silas in disbelief. His apology seemed genuine, which was a word she would have never previously chosen to describe him. For a moment, she wondered if the photo incident really inspired regret in Silas, or was this just some attempt to try to trick her into something? Mulling this over, she watched as Toby continued to hug Silas's neck, his sweet giggles never ceasing. Silas smiled too, though he appeared to be limiting the full scale of his grin.

Had she been too harsh on him? Leah wondered as a wisp of guilt breezed into her heart like a single autumn leaf. Something about his sincere words and Toby's obvious affection for him put a sizable crack in the wall she'd built. *Am I judging a man's entire worth by the mistakes of his youth?*

Silas glanced over his shoulder when he heard his customers exit the shop, chatting about the purchases they'd made. They stopped to pet Willow once more, who woke from her sunbathing and eagerly received their head scratches and chin rubs.

Silas turned back to Leah and gently transferred Toby into her arms. "I know that our business relationship got off on the wrong foot and that's my fault." He rubbed the palms of his hands together as if generating the fortitude to say more. "If it's *oll recht* with you, I'd like to set up a time for us to talk and figure out how we can better work together."

Another surprise! Silas was treating her kindly, but she'd never imagined that he would go through the trouble of setting up some sort of meeting to hash out their differences. The idea of being alone with him caused her heart to race and her forehead to perspire. Could she trust that he had good intentions?

Swallowing against the lump that had formed in her throat, Leah nodded in agreement. "Wh-where should we meet?"

"I've always enjoyed meals at the Bird-in-Hand Family Restaurant. Would you like to have dinner there?" Silas asked with an unmistakable sparkle in his ocean-blue eyes.

"Jah," Leah hesitantly agreed, hoping she wasn't stepping into a trap. "Wh-when?"

"How 'bout Saturday night? The roadside stand closes at five o'clock, *jah*? I could pick you up at seven. That will give us time to close our businesses."

"Nee, I'll borrow my *daed*'s buggy and m-meet you there," Leah responded. She refused to subject herself to a potentially awkward buggy ride with Silas, just as she had declined his offer of a ride home from the church gathering for the same reason. This would be her first time socializing with him for more than a few minutes, and she wanted to have the option to leave on her own accord should things turn sour.

"That's fine with me. We'll meet at the restaurant at seven o'clock," he replied.

Leah nodded. "I better get back to w-work." As she turned to leave, she thanked the tourists for visiting, including the woman who had taken Toby's photo, though she felt as if she was walking through a thick fog. Toby snuggled into her chest as she carried him back toward the shop, feeling dizzier with each step she took.

"Wh-what a day," she said to Toby. First, the early arrival of Silas and his tourists, then the sudden rush in the shop, then that woman taking Toby's picture, and to top it all off, Silas Riehl asking her to dinner.

Though there were plenty of cars still in the parking lot, which let Leah know that the shop was still busy, she felt the need to sit down.

Fighting a sudden sense of exhaustion, Leah pondered her situation. Never in her wildest dreams did she imagine she would willingly go on an outing with Silas. If someone had predicted the future and had told her that it would happen, she would have laughed in their face. She reminded herself that getting along with her former enemy was a blessing, though the pain of her past taunted her not to believe this. She sighed heavily, knowing that letting go of her fear and learning to trust Silas would be no easy task.

* * *

At the end of the day, after the last buggy ride had been given and all the horses were thoroughly cared for and released into the grazing pasture, Silas sat in his business shed with the cashbox in front of him. He counted the money in the metal box, picked up his pen to record the totals in his ledger, then paused. He realized he'd been lost in thought as he'd counted the neatly organized bills and had no idea how much cash had been brought in that day.

I can't believe I asked Leah out to supper, and that she agreed to go with me, he thought, picking up the stack of bills to count them again. *It's my one chance to work things out with her and make sure that the addition of farm tours is a permanent part of my business.*

Silas groaned, looking down again at the bills in his hand. He'd counted them again without paying attention.

"All the gear is put away and the buggies and wagons have been washed. I'm *hungerich*, so I'm heading home for supper," Ivan said cheerfully as he stepped up to the booth.

Silas flinched, startled by Ivan's sudden appearance.

Ivan threw his head back and guffawed. "Did I scare ya?"

"*Jah*, my head is just somewhere else I guess," Silas replied as he started to count the money for the third time.

"Well, where's it at?"

"What?"

"Your head," Ivan teased. "I can see Leah didn't bite it off when you took the tourists out to the Fisher farm, so it must be around here somewhere."

"Hilarious," Silas responded dryly. He had too much on his mind and didn't have the energy to laugh at Ivan's joke.

"Speaking of Leah," Ivan said as he leaned against the shed, "the idea to take the rides to her roadside stand and tour the Fisher farm was very *schmart*. Six of the seven groups I had today chose the farm tour, so it's clear that the tourists love it."

"*Jah*, it does seem popular," Silas agreed, though his enthusiasm was dulled by his concerns.

If he and Leah couldn't find a way to get along and work together, she might put a stop to the farm tours, and that would hurt his growing business. What a shame that would be.

He let out a weary sigh. Then he thanked and said goodbye to Ivan before putting the money back in his cashbox. He would count it again in the morning. Hopefully, he'd be able to focus then.

I'll have to pray about this meeting with Leah, Silas firmly resolved, knowing that everything, including their tumultuous relationship, was in the Creator's hands.

Chapter Eight

Silas could have kicked himself when he checked the inexpensive pocket watch that he kept inside his buggy. It was ten minutes past seven, and he was late. He scolded himself as he tied his horse to the hitching rail outside of the Bird-in-Hand Family Restaurant. After years of receiving the cold shoulder from Leah, this was perhaps his only chance to redeem himself to her. Silas knew he had a lot to atone for and didn't want to give Leah anything else to hold against him, especially something as silly as tardiness. This date had to go perfectly.

Date? This wasn't a date. Silas firmly reminded himself that Leah didn't even want to ride with him to the restaurant. This was just a friendly dinner so they could talk business and hopefully iron out their differences.

He darted through the restaurant doors and

then sprinted up the small set of stairs before arriving in the lobby. The area was busy with lots of people milling about, most of whom were *Englischers* who browsed through the restaurant's small gift shop. Silas moved through the crowd, his eyes scanning the room as he searched for Leah.

When his eyes finally landed on her, his heart skipped a beat. Leah was sharing a seat on one of the numerous benches with an elderly *Englisch* couple. She smiled as she chatted with them, looking as lovely as that evening's colorful sunset. She wore a typical black cape apron over a plum-colored dress that brought out her hazel eyes. Her thick, dark brunette hair was neatly parted and styled into the traditional bun at the nape of her neck, which was covered by her heart-shaped *kapp*. Silas admitted to himself that Leah was the most beautiful woman in the room, even though she was dressed so plainly.

She noticed Silas approaching and rose from her seat. "Hiya, Silas. *Wie b-bischt?*"

Silas took off his straw hat and held it at his side. "Doing real *gut, denki* for asking. I hope you are too." He nodded a greeting at the couple before speaking again. "I'm sorry to be running late."

The tiniest smile that Silas had ever seen

crossed Leah's lips. "Th-that's *oll recht*. There's a fifteen-minute wait to be s-seated. I g-gave the hostess my name to add to the l-list."

"Still, I hope I didn't keep you waiting long." Silas felt a weight lift from his shoulders. Even though he'd been feeling hunger pains for several hours, the unexpected delay in seating was a blessing.

Leah nodded, but she didn't respond. She moved her purse strap from one shoulder to the other as she glanced around the room, avoiding eye contact with him.

"This is a popular place," said the elderly gentleman seated on the bench. "That old saying must be true. The best things in life are worth waiting for." He stretched his right arm and wrapped it around the woman's shoulders. "My wife takes so long to get ready that I have fallen asleep waiting for her."

The woman's mouth dropped open and she gave the man a push with her unsteady hand. "You must not mind, since we've been married for fifty-four years!"

The man threw his head back and let out a deep chuckle. Then turning his attention to Leah, he spoke again. "If history repeats itself and this young fellow is always running late, you two will probably be hitched and playfully bickering for over fifty years as well."

Leah's cheeks reddened and she dropped her gaze. Silas couldn't tell if she was amused by the sentiment or if she was embarrassed that the man assumed they were a couple.

"We'd like to welcome Leah, party of two," a voice called from the hostess's podium.

As if waiting for the perfect moment to escape, Leah hurried toward the voice without waiting for Silas.

Something about the awkward situation made Silas grin. He said goodbye to the *Englisch* couple and then dashed to catch up with Leah.

Soon the unlikely pair were seated at a comfortable booth near one of the many windows. Silas glanced up from his menu a few times to gauge Leah's mood. She certainly didn't seem as uncomfortable as she usually did in his presence. Still, he sensed she was guarded. *Progress is progress*, Silas thought, deciding not to read into Leah's every move.

He cleared his throat. "Are you thinking of having the buffet, or are you gonna order something off the menu?"

Leah looked up from her menu and glanced longingly toward the smorgasbord. "It's hard to ch-choose. Wh-what are you gonna have?"

Silas smiled, pleased to be having a civil conversation with her. "I'm real *hungerich* so

I'm leaning toward the buffet. Anyone who is filling their plates over there better get out of the way when I come over." He wiggled his eyebrows, hoping to make Leah smile, but to his disappointment, she returned her gaze to her menu.

A few moments later, a middle-aged *Englisch* waitress approached their table to take their orders. Silas said he'd like to eat from the buffet and asked for a root beer. Leah ordered a roasted turkey sandwich and a side of fries, along with an iced tea.

As soon as the waitress hurried back to the kitchen, a few minutes of painfully awkward silence landed on the table between them. Silas looked around the restaurant, wanting to allow Leah to speak first. She quietly gazed out the window, the amber glow of the sunset kissing her cheeks.

Eventually, she turned her attention to him. "Aren't you g-gonna go up to the buffet?"

Silas shook his head. "I'll wait until your food arrives so we can eat together."

Leah nodded and then began to fiddle with her silverware.

Silas opened his mouth to say something more, but his nerves prevented words from leaving his mouth. Should he apologize for his boyhood actions that so deeply hurt her, or would it be better to simply let go of the past and move forward? Or did his childhood mean streak permanently ruin any chance he might have at a friendship with this smart, lovely, hardworking woman?

The waitress returned to the table with their beverages. When Silas reached for his glass, his nerves got the best of him. His trembling hand bumped the glass, which sent a current of soda splashing onto his shirt and trousers.

"That was graceful," he sarcastically complimented himself, though he was thankful that the beverage hadn't tipped over in Leah's direction. Scrambling for some napkins, Silas began to sop up the spill when he heard Leah giggling. She covered her grin with her slender hand, shielding her pretty smile. "What's so funny?" he asked, his coy smile daring her to admit that she was laughing at him.

Leah handed Silas her napkin so he could finish cleaning up the spill. "Just m-made me think that this isn't the only time that you s-spilled something and caused a s-scene."

Silas wadded all the soaking napkins together at the end of the table. "When was that?" His interest was piqued, and he thoroughly enjoyed having such a normal conversation with Leah.

She looked at him as if he'd lost his mind.

"Don't you r-remember the last day of first grade, when it was so hot and humid in the *schul haus*?"

"Jah," Silas replied slowly, trying to piece together what Leah was getting at.

"You spilled your b-bottle of water all over yourself during l-lunch, and then you t-told everyone you'd done that on p-purpose just to cool off." Leah's eyes pinched shut and her hand returned to her face to hide her chuckles. "Then you turned r-red and hid in the outhouse."

Silas scratched his head and let out a laugh that was a little too loud. "I can't believe you remember that." He cringed at the embarrassing memory.

Leah was quite clearly biting her tongue to keep the volume of her laughter at an acceptable level. "That was p-pretty hard to forget."

The server, noticing the aftermath of the spill, approached the table with a damp rag to wipe away the stickiness of the soda and provided the table with more napkins. When she left, taking the damp napkins with her, Silas took a deep breath. Thankful that the proverbial ice had been broken by his beverage mishap, he felt this was the right time to apologize for being the menace that he'd been during his youth.

"Leah, I'm awful sorry about how I treated you when we were *kinner.* I never meant to actually hurt you." He looked her in the eyes as he atoned for his behavior, but soon the heaviness of his guilt forced him to stare down at the table. "If I'd only realized how much my words affected you, I would've never been so cruel."

"Okay," came Leah's soft voice from across the table.

"I promise you," he pressed on, reaching for her hand, "I will never let you down again."

Leah's eyes grew large as pumpkins as Silas continued to hold her hand from across the table. Had she felt that same spark that he had when their hands touched?

Silas was tickled pink when Leah didn't immediately pull her hand away. Once again, he briefly considered how very easily he could develop a serious romantic interest in her. Her gentle ways and hardworking spirit were very attractive, as was her lovely face. Silas had to admit to himself that he had a newfound crush on Leah.

He released her hand and then cleared his throat, still processing the surprising amount of chemistry that their innocent touch had mustered. "Now that we're on the same page, let's discuss our businesses. Tell me about your schedule."

The pair discussed their establishments and determined where potential problems might arise. Leah explained that her roadside stand was open Monday through Saturday between nine and five. Silas shared how Riehl's Buggy Rides was open during the same days but was open to visitors an hour earlier, so he agreed not to offer farm tours until nine o'clock. Leah also told Silas that she was having difficulty keeping up with the demand for her baked goods with the influx of new customers. Together they came up with the idea for Leah to close the roadside stand on Mondays, historically the slowest day for her business. This would allow her an entire day to focus on replenishing her supply of baked items.

By the time the server returned to the table with a replacement soda for Silas and Leah's meal, the unlikely pair had figured out a plethora of different ways to improve their experience while working together.

As Silas left the table and took his place in the small line near the buffet, he forced himself to take several deep breaths. *This evening is going far better than I was expecting*, he thought as he filled his plate with fried chicken, buttered noodles, mashed potatoes, carrots, corn and two dinner rolls. *If things continue*

*to go well with Leah, eventually I might even
ask if she would allow me to court her.*

As he headed back to the table with his
nearly overflowing plate, Silas mentally shook
himself to clear his mind. It was far too soon to
think about the very minuscule chance that he
would ever get close to Leah. For now, he just
needed to be thankful for the progress their
relationship had made tonight.

Leah stared at her untouched meal as she
waited for Silas to return from the buffet. Her
stomach lurched with pangs of hunger. She'd
been so nervous about tonight's meeting that
she'd barely eaten a morsel throughout the day.
Now that evening was here and things seemed
to be going well between them, she was starting to relax. Only now did she realize the full
extent of her hunger.

When Silas returned to the table, they bowed
their heads in silent prayer.

When he lifted his gaze, Silas rubbed his
hands together briskly in anticipation of the
savory meal that he was about to devour. "This
looks *wunderbaar gut*!" he exclaimed as he
took a bite of the fried chicken. "Tell me, what
gave you the idea to start a roadside stand?"
he asked around a mouthful of food.

Leah picked up her sandwich, savoring the

smoky scent of the roasted turkey. "I always liked b-baking." She took a dainty bite of the sandwich, not wanting to appear ravenously unladylike.

"So, you thought a roadside stand would be a good outlet for that hobby?"

"*Jah*. My p-parents and older *schwester* thought having a b-business of my own would t-take my mind off my anxiety p-problem," Leah replied as she dipped one of her crispy fries into some ketchup.

When she realized what she'd just said, she dropped the ketchup-covered fry onto her plate. Why in the world had she shared that personal detail with Silas? He already probably assumed that she was the nervous sort, and she didn't need to give him anything else to tease her over.

As suddenly as she'd had this thought, a feeling of guilt swept over her. Silas was acting friendly and sociable, and he'd apologized for his boyhood actions. If she was being honest with herself, he hadn't done or said anything unkind since they graduated from the one-room schoolhouse when they were fourteen. Was it fair for her to assume he was still up to no good?

Silas buttered one of his dinner rolls and nodded. "I understand. Running a business certainly takes up a lot of one's time. It's worth it though, *jah*?"

Leah agreed silently with a single nod.

"And it's such a *schee* little shop that you have," he went on as he shook some salt onto his food. "What do you sell the most of?"

She munched on a few of her fries before answering. She wasn't used to talking about herself, especially with someone whom she wasn't very close with. "In the s-summertime, the produce from my *mamm*'s garden sells out d-daily. Martha's j-jams and jellies are popular all year round, and so are F-Fern's quilted items."

"What about your baked goods? As tasty as they are, I imagine they sell like hotcakes."

Leah stared at her glass of iced tea, slowly stirring the liquid with her straw. It almost felt like Silas was being overly pleasant. It was such a stark contrast to her memories of how he'd acted in the past that his current warmth put her on edge.

"They also sell p-pretty well," she finally answered, hoping she didn't sound like she was boasting.

"*Ach*, of course. You're baking is the best I've ever tasted, and I'm sure your skills earn you wagonloads of repeat customers," Silas replied. He smiled at her before he paused to fork some noodles into his mouth.

"D-denki," Leah answered quietly. She hoped that this was the end of his chain of compliments. If his words were true, she appreciated them. If they weren't, they served as nothing more than a failed attempt to butter her up.

His knife clinked against the plate as he cut a large chunk of carrot in half, seemingly unaware that the metallic scraping sound was causing her to cringe.

"Jah, Leah's Countryside Cupboard has everything a shopper could ever want—high-quality, locally made and grown items, the tastiest baked goods in Lancaster County, and a nice owner to greet her customers."

Leah couldn't stand his pandering for a moment longer. She leaned over her plate and stared him down across the table. "You think I'm nice? We've b-barely had a conversation in which I wasn't y-yelling at you or accusing you of something."

His mouth twisted to one side and his shoulders fell. *"Jah*, I do think you're nice." He stared out the window beside their table, as if he couldn't bring himself to look her in the eye. "Maybe you haven't been real cordial with me, but it's not like you didn't have a reason."

Leah sat back in her seat, relaxing against the booth. She hadn't expected his vulnerable reaction. Her initial suspicion might have been justified considering their past, but her conscience would not allow her to ignore his sincere look of regret. *Becoming friends with Silas will be more difficult than I expected*, Leah thought as she realized she would always have to fight feelings of mistrust toward him.

"I'm s-s-sorry," Leah said, stumbling over her words. Never in her wildest dreams did she believe she would be the one apologizing. It was more likely to snow on the fourth of July.

Silas returned his gaze to her, his bruised expression mellowing. "That's okay, Leah." A thoughtful smile illuminated his face. "It will take time for things to feel comfortable between us, but I'm more than willing to be patient."

Leah's breath caught in her throat. "*D-denki* for that," she replied. She stared down at her meal, unable to look at Silas for a moment longer, not with the sweet way he was smiling at her.

The pair enjoyed the rest of their meal in silence, though Leah talked to the Lord in the solitude of her heart. She thanked *Gott* that the evening had turned out better than anticipated, and asked for the strength and wisdom to figure out who Silas truly was.

Chapter Nine

The late-September weather turned unseasonably hot and muggy by the following Tuesday. Leah kept busy in the roadside stand, but sticky weather seemed to keep the usual flock of customers away. However, she didn't truly mind the lull in business. She was thankful to have the time to sweep and mop the floor, dust the shelves, and take inventory of the items she had for sale.

When it was time for a lunch break, Leah walked across the shop and took a seat on the stool that she kept behind the counter. She opened the small cooler that she'd packed for lunch and took out the ham and cheese sandwich, though the intense heat had stolen most of her appetite. As she nibbled on her lunch, she eyed the pecan pie she had tucked away in the cubby beneath the counter. She'd baked that pie for Silas as a gesture of goodwill, and she looked forward to offering him this tasty token of kindness. He seemed to be making a sincere effort to repair their relationship, and she now felt obligated to do the same.

When her lunch was about half-eaten, the shop door suddenly swished open, causing the small bell above the door to almost jingle off its hook. Fern stepped in, red in the face and forehead shiny with perspiration. She hurried toward the counter and placed down her armload of lap quilts. "For goodness' sake, I feel like I just walked across the surface of the sun!"

Leah chuckled, enjoying Fern's animated ways. "Help yourself to a c-cool drink," she offered, gesturing toward the propane-powered refrigerator.

Fern thanked her and scurried across the store, retrieved a bottle of homemade lemonade, then promptly returned to the counter. She quickly removed the bottle's cap and drank most of the refreshing liquid, then took a deep breath while pressing the chilled bottle against her cheeks.

"You sh-should've waited until evening to bring these over," Leah gently scolded her friend, concerned for Fern's wellbeing. "No need to have ridden your s-scooter in the heat of the d-day."

Fern drank down the last of the lemonade before a mischievous smile spread across her flushed face. "Well, restocking these lap quilts gave me the perfect excuse to come and visit. I would've ridden my scooter across the desert just to hear about your date with Silas."

Leah playfully scoffed. "So, there's an ulterior m-motive, *jah*?"

Fern planted one hand on her hip and used her other hand to shake her finger at Leah. "Don't try to change the subject! Tell me, how was your date with Silas?"

Leah took the last bite of her sandwich to buy herself some time, then tossed the aluminum foil wrapping into the wastebasket that she hid behind the counter. "It was not a d-date," she replied, wondering what would have given Fern that impression. "We met so we could move past our d-differences and figure out how we can w-work together."

Fern's expression softened as if she realized the topic was sensitive. "Do you think you can work together?"

Leah's lips formed a small grin as she used her handkerchief to dab some sweat from the back of her neck. "I th-think so. He apologized for b-bullying me when we were *kinner*." Hearing Silas's sincere apology for his past actions gave her hope that he wouldn't pick on her again. She wasn't going to tell anyone, even Fern, about the butterflies that she'd felt when Silas held her hand so gently. Truth be told, she'd never experienced that feeling before. She determinedly forced herself to shrug it off, attributing the fluttering sensation to simply being nervous.

"That's *wunderbaar gut*," Fern gushed, still rolling the cool lemonade bottle over her face. "I don't think I've ever seen you smile when talking about Silas!"

Before Leah could deny that Silas brought her any amount of happiness and that it was making peace with him that made her smile, Fern spoke up again.

"I'm so glad it worked out for you! Who knows, maybe you and Silas will even be friends someday!"

"I d-doubt it," Leah disagreed, her grin fading. "T-too much damage has been done in the past. I don't think I could ever t-trust him, but I'm glad we can get along at least. That's what really m-matters."

The brightness of Fern's grin suddenly didn't reach her eyes. "You're right, getting along is enough for now. I suppose you can't rush this sort of thing."

The bell above the door jingled again, causing both women to turn. A group of tourists filed into the shop and greeted the Amish women excitedly before they started to browse. Fern and Leah resumed their conversation while the *Englischers* shopped, but they were interrupted when the door swung open again and Silas stepped inside, looking all done in. Though his skin had a healthy bronze glow from all his time spent outdoors, he seemed quite red in the face. Several damp patches on his navy-blue shirt showed his perspiration. In this weather, it certainly didn't take long to work up a sweat, which he had done while getting his team of horses several pails of cool water to enjoy as they rested.

"Looks like you're about to be pretty busy so I'll be on my way," Fern said coyly. She tilted her head in Silas's direction. "Try to stay cool. *Mache gut.*"

Leah bid her friend farewell, grinning at Fern's gentle warning. Fern had nothing to worry about, as long as Silas remained cordial. Leah glanced again at the pie that she would soon give to him. It felt good to be doing her part to keep the peace between them, and hopefully, Silas would continue to do the same.

Several minutes passed as the buggy ride group browsed through the roadside stand, lined up at the register to pay for their purchases, then exited the building. When the last of the tourists exited the shop through the back door and made their way to the picnic tables, Silas stepped up and placed a chilled pint of lemonade on the counter.

"Guder m-mariye," Leah greeted him politely, using a clean cloth to wipe away the excess condensation that had already accumulated on the side of the glass bottle. "M-muggy day, *jah*?"

Silas nodded in agreement and sighed. "I need something cool to drink so I don't melt. I don't mind saying that I'm not fond of this weather."

"I don't m-mind it so much," Leah replied with a quick shrug. "Better than being s-snowed in."

Silas harrumphed. "At least one can escape the cold by going indoors. The only way to escape this heat would be if I walked outside, took one of my horse's buckets of water, and poured it over my head."

Leah chuckled at the thought of Silas purposely drenching himself.

Silas, however, didn't crack a smile. Apparently, the heat had him in no joking mood.

Understanding that not everyone enjoyed such weather, Leah brushed off the awkward moment. "W-would you like a snack to g-go with your drink?"

"*Nee*, just the lemonade."

Leah was a little surprised to hear him turn down a treat, especially since he had claimed to enjoy her baking so much. Had he been lying about that, or was the heat just making him grumpy?

When he nudged the bottle toward her and reached for his wallet, she held up her hand to stop him. "There's no ch-charge when you bring me c-customers, remember?"

"*Ach*, that's right. *Denki*." Silas reached for the bottle, removed the lid, and took a long drink.

"You may not want a s-snack now, but I have a gift for you that you can t-take home and enjoy later," Leah said. She bent to retrieve the pie that had been waiting for him. "I m-made this for you."

Silas looked astonished when Leah placed the pie in his hands. "Wow, *denki*, Leah. I wasn't expecting anything like this." He held the pie up for closer inspection, sniffed it, then grimaced.

"*W-was iss letz?*" Leah asked, feeling her chest tighten as Silas stared at the pie with an increasing look of disapproval.

"Nothing's wrong," Silas replied, his already flushed face deepening to a nearly magenta color.

She wasn't buying his response. "You m-made a face."

"*Nee*, I didn't."

"*Jah*, you d-did."

"I did not."

"You're f-frowning r-right n-now!" Leah exhaled forcefully. Her frustration with Silas made her kitten of a stutter turn into a lion. She was under the impression that they were trying to get along now, and here he was making things difficult yet again. At least he could be honest about his obvious rejection of her gift!

"*Ach*, I'm sorry, Leah. I don't think I can accept this pie. Maybe you can share it with your *familye* or sell it to one of your customers." He held the pie out, waiting for her to take it back.

Leah was so stunned by his refusal of her gift, as well as his suggestion to give it to someone else, that she had to take a moment to process what he'd said. "You'd r-rather I sell it?"

He bobbed his head. "*Jah*, I think that would be best." He looked at the pie again and scrunched his face.

Leah was flabbergasted.

Silas inched closer toward the counter, still holding the pie out to her.

Instead of accepting it, she planted her hands

on her hips. "Th-this is *narrish*! I sh-should've known that you would r-react like this."

Silas placed the pie on the counter. "Hold on now, if you would—"

"Nee!" Leah cut him off, her tone as sharp as a blade as she pointed an accusing finger in his direction. "I can't b-believe how *narrish* I was to th-think that we c-could get along. Th-this is what I get for t-trying to be n-neighborly toward you."

His eyes landed on the nearby open window. "Maybe lower your voice. Folks might hear you."

Leah was about to snap back that she could act however she wanted to in her own shop but stopped herself before the angry words left her mouth. It was true; the tourists didn't need and probably wouldn't want to hear a heated argument.

Instead, she let out an exasperated grumble. "You c-could have at least been p-polite about not w-wanting the pie instead of m-making a face at it." She grabbed the pie and then carried it to the refrigerator, placing it beside the other pies that were for sale.

Silas followed her across the store. "Hang on, it's not that I don't appreciate—"

"If you appreciated it, you wouldn't have looked like I was giving you a handful of wworms," she interrupted, slamming the refrigerator door shut.

He released an agitated sigh, still standing in his spot near the counter. "If you would just give me a minute to explain—"

"I don't w-want to hear it," she interjected, feeling quite done with their conversation. A trickle of sweat ran down her neck. Perhaps the scorching weather was getting to her now as well.

Silas balled his fingers into fists. "Fine, then don't listen!" With that, he turned on his heels and stomped out of the shop, his heavy footsteps rattling some of her merchandise that was displayed on shelves near the doors.

Leah dashed to the window and watched as Silas stomped toward his waiting horses. She threw her hands in the air and grumbled loudly, glad that no one was around to hear her miffed outburst. She seethed with irritation, so much so that she felt her entire body trembling as if she'd spent too much time outdoors on a chilly winter day.

This is what I get for thinking that Silas and I could work things out. I try to be nice to him, and he throws my kindness back in my face, Leah thought, fuming as she replayed their interaction in her mind. Just when she thought things were starting to work out between her and her lifelong enemy, once again, she felt embarrassed and anxious. *For sure and for certain*, she thought with resentment, *Silas and I will never see eye to eye.*

I've never met someone so stubborn in my life, Silas grumbled to himself as he stomped to his waiting horse and wagon. He gracelessly launched himself into the driver's seat of the wagon, jostling the rig so much that the gelding issued an annoyed whinny.

"She just can't give me the benefit of the doubt," Silas said aloud with only the horses to hear his frustrations. He was glad that his buggy ride customers were still seated on the picnic benches that were located on the other side of the shop. They didn't need to overhear his frustrated outburst. His fists balled so tightly that his fingernails dug into his calloused palms. "It's always been a matter of if she could work with me. *Vell*, maybe I can't work with her."

Silas stared at the roadside stand, and the longer he glared at the quaint shop, the more he felt like calling off the farm tours just so he wouldn't have to deal with Leah's relentless skepticism.

He jumped down from the wagon and marched toward the shop so he could go back in and tell Leah that she would never have to deal with him or the extra customers he brought her ever again. He made it halfway across the parking lot when Willow bounded up to him, wagging her tail and woofing a greeting.

He sighed and stopped to pet the loving canine. As the dog looked up at him with expressive, friendly eyes, Silas started to calm down and allowed himself to think rationally. Putting a halt to the farm tours would not only affect Leah's profits but would disturb his income as well.

Besides, he reasoned with himself as he stroked the dog's velvety ears, Leah was still learning to trust him. Maybe he should go back inside, apologize, and explain to her why he didn't accept her gift.

He looked up when he heard a chorus of voices and was disappointed to see that his customers were approaching him, refreshed and ready to continue their tour of the countryside. Silas didn't want to inconvenience his guests by asking them to wait while he hashed things out with Leah, nor did he want them to overhear should a shouting match break out.

Making up with Leah, for what felt like the tenth time, would have to wait for another occasion.

Chapter Ten

Leah made a trip to the local bulk foods store on the following Monday afternoon. The unusual autumn heatwave had finally broken, and with the cooler weather, she quite enjoyed the half hour buggy ride to the quaint grocery shop. After finishing her baking that morning, she noticed her supplies were running low. Knowing she wouldn't have enough materials when it came time to bake again the next week, she decided to get the errand done. The peaceful, well-organized bulk foods store was Amish-owned and operated, so she felt right at home as she strolled down the neat aisles, filling up her cart and checking items off her shopping list.

As Leah exited the store with two large paper bags cradled in her arms, she noticed a group of young *Englisch* men. They stood clustered beside her buggy, and as she approached, she soon determined they couldn't be more than seventeen or eighteen years old. Although the shop was well-hidden deep in the country-side and was visited by mostly Amish custom-ers, tourists occasionally stopped in to pick up some snacks to enjoy during their travels.

Assuming the young fellows were simply curious about her plain mode of transportation, Leah strolled across the parking lot, hoping the group would leave by the time she reached the hitching rail.

"Excuse m-me," she stuttered when she reached the back of the buggy. She hoped this polite nudge would give the guys a hint that they needed to move on.

The young men looked in her direction and grinned, though something about their smiles didn't sit right with Leah.

"Is this your horse?" one of the young men asked. He wore sunglasses and had a cigarette hanging out of his mouth that danced from one side to the other as he spoke.

"*Jah*, sh-she is," Leah answered, readjusting her grip on her heavy shopping bags. "If you'll excuse me, I n-need to g-get going." Truthfully, she was in no rush and had no other plans for the rest of the afternoon, but something about these fellows set her on edge.

The second guy, who was taller and more muscular than the first, took a step closer to Leah. "Don't be in such a hurry. We'd like to go for a horse and carriage ride."

The third fellow, who wore his hair in a long, slick ponytail, snickered at that.

Leah felt her face grow warm. Something was definitely off about these people; she knew it in her gut. She glanced around the parking lot hoping to see another person who might help her escape her predicament, but only her buggy and a single red van were in the store's parking lot.

She held in a sigh and reluctantly responded to the stranger's bizarre request. "Th-there are s-several places that offer buggy rides around Lancaster C-County. I can r-recommend one to you." She planned to suggest one of the tours located in nearby Intercourse or Strasburg because she didn't want to risk Silas unknowingly bringing these creepy guys to her home.

The guy with the sunglasses and the cigarette hanging out of his mouth, who seemed to be the leader of the group, cackled at Leah's suggestion. "Why would we pay for a buggy ride when we can take a free one right now?"

Leah didn't respond. She felt her heart jump into her throat when the ringleader hopped into her buggy. He fiddled with the side mirror so he could see her from inside the rig. Were these unsettling strangers planning on stealing her horse and buggy?

"I—I—I need to l-leave now," Leah said, shivering as she hugged her grocery bags tightly.

The muscular fellow let out a whoop and jumped into the buggy next to his smoking friend. One of the troublemakers picked up the reins and gave a hard tug. Their noisy, boisterous behavior and their unfamiliar handling of the reins spooked the mare, who whinnied and began to nervously stomp in place.

If only I'd brought Willow along for the ride, Leah thought. These rude people would probably think twice about getting into her buggy with a protective dog barking at them. She started to worry that someone was about to get hurt, so she approached the horse to calm it down.

The long-haired man moved to block her path. "Let us take your horse and buggy out for a spin. We'll promise to come right back."

Leah felt her hands begin to tremble, wondering how she would ever get away from this terrible group. "P-please leave me alone," she begged the *Englischers*. "You're s-scaring my h-horse. I don't w-want anyone to get hurt!"

The hooligans ignored her, two of them

continuing to sit in and rummage through her buggy, while the long-haired man approached the hitching rail. Was he about to untie her horse?

"Please, horses can s-spook around unfamiliar p-people!"

"What's s-s-spooky is that s-s-stutter," jeered the ringleader of the group, mocking Leah's speech problem.

The rest of the young men burst into fits of laughter at the ringleader's cruel antics.

Hot tears burned Leah's eyes and it took every ounce of her strength to keep them at bay. "P-please g-g-go."

"Oh, we'll go," said the long-haired man, "but we're taking your carriage with us."

"Yeah," the ringleader gleefully agreed as he grabbed the reins from his friend. "Let's get going so we can get back before sunset."

The long-haired man moved to squeeze into the buggy beside his two friends just as Leah darted forward to grab the reins from the strangers. They collided, causing her to drop her bags of groceries. All the items she had purchased spilled out and the large flour bag burst when it hit the pavement, sending the white powder in all directions.

Humiliated and panicking, Leah started to cry. She dropped to the ground, tearing a hole in her wine-colored dress when her knees skidded against the pavement. She grasped the paper bags and then scrambled to collect her scattered, partially damaged groceries. She called out to her Heavenly Father from her panicked heart. *Please send someone to help me!*

"Hey! What's going on here?"

Leah turned and felt a wave of relief at the sound of a familiar male voice. It was Silas, and he was rushing toward her. Amid the commotion, and in her distressed state, she hadn't noticed his buggy pull into the store's parking lot. A rescuer had arrived.

Silas extended both hands to Leah, pulling her to her feet. "Are you hurt?" His eyes shone with alarm, and concern etched deeply across his suntanned face.

She started to answer but became so tonguetied on the first syllable of her response that she couldn't answer.

"It's *oll recht*," Silas whispered calmly, using his thumbs to gently wipe away her tears, "I'm here now. I've got you."

Without realizing what she was doing, Leah wrapped her arms around Silas and clung to him tightly as she tried to gain control of her emotions. She'd never been so happy to see a familiar face, even if it belonged to a person she had despised not that long ago. No matter what happened next, she knew she was safe. At that moment, being held by Silas felt like her prayer was answered.

After the brief but powerful embrace, Silas's expression became very stern as he turned his attention to the band of young men. "What's all this about?" He demanded an answer, his tone as rigid as a lightning bolt.

"We're just trying to make friends," said the ringleader, who had previously pretended to be the toughest.

"Friends? Seems to me that you were harassing this woman," Silas retorted, crossing his arms over his chest. He took a few steps closer to the *Englischers*. "Where are your parents?"

The muscular young man, who seemed like he still had some fight left in him, scoffed at Silas's question. "Why?"

"I'm going to have a word with them," Silas replied calmly but firmly, maintaining unwavering eye contact with the defiant young man.

"They're not here," the long-haired kid spoke up.

Silas craned his neck around the rowdy group and pointed toward a red van that was parked on the other side of the lot. "Then get in your car and leave," he said, calling the group's bluff.

The trio nervously exchanged glances before the ringleader sighed. "My parents are in the store. They have the keys."

A small glint of compassion sparkled in Silas's eyes. "Look, I understand what it's like to be young and carefree. But there's never any reason to tease someone to this point." He motioned toward Leah as she dabbed at her red nose. "This wasn't good-hearted fun. This was cruel. You need to apologize to my friend, replace her damaged things, and then ask the shopkeepers for a broom and dustpan to sweep up this flour."

The ringleader looked somewhat repentant, but the muscular guy and the long-haired one remained stubborn.

"Or what? What are you gonna do about it, Amish dude?" the long-haired boy asked as the muscular one chuckled.

Silas shrugged and glanced toward the store. "Our people usually don't like to get involved with nonsense like this, but I have no problem talking to your parents. Shouldn't be hard to pick them out since there's only one vehicle here."

"All right, all right," the muscular kid agreed, holding his hands up in surrender. "Listen, ma'am, we're sorry for acting like jerks. We were just trying to have some fun and got carried away."

Leah, still shaking, couldn't form the words to respond. She nodded, picked up her groceries that had survived the fall, and slumped into her buggy. As she sat inside, hiding from the world, Silas followed the boys to the front porch of the store and waited outside until they returned with a replacement bag of flour, a broom, and a dustpan. They swept up the mess on the pavement and returned the cleaning supplies to the store, then congregated near the car until the adults exited the shop.

As the car pulled away, Silas approached Leah's buggy. He set the replacement flour on the passenger's seat, then walked around to the driver's side, where Leah sat. "They're gone," he kindly reassured her. "Are you *oll recht*?"

Leah took a shaky breath and wiped her eyes. "*J-jah*. I was so s-scared. I d-don't know what I w-would've done if you hadn't sh-shown up."

Silas nodded understandingly. "I don't think they would've really stolen your *gaul* and buggy, but I can imagine how scary that must have been." He looked down at his work boots like he was unsure if he should say what was on his mind. "You would've been fine even if no one showed up." He looked up and gazed into Leah's watery eyes with a warmth she didn't recognize. "You are a lot stronger than you give yourself credit for. Plus, the Lord is always with you, and if you'll let me, I will be too."

Leah studied Silas's sincere expression as she processed his comforting words. Who was this young man that she was looking at? Had that bothersome, antagonizing boy she'd known her entire life grown into someone whom she could call a friend?

Silas cleared his throat and pointed to Leah's shaking hands. "You're too upset to take your *gaul* out on the road right now." Using his thumb, he gestured to the nearby road. "There's an ice cream place nearby. Let's go have some, my treat. We can sit there for a bit until you're feeling better. Maybe we can also talk about the little spat we had last week."

Leah shook her head and dabbed at her eyes with the corner of her apron. She was somewhat ashamed of the scene that Silas had rescued her from, and she didn't want to take up more of his time. "*Nee*, I'm f-fine. *Denki*, though."

"*Ach*, c'mon. No one in their right mind says no to ice cream," Silas insisted as his mouth formed a hopeful smile. "We can take my buggy."

Leah looked down at her clothing, noticing the tear in the skirt of her dress. Flour still clung to her black apron as if she'd been busy baking up a storm in the kitchen and had left her house without taking the time to clean up.

Embarrassed by her unintentionally unkempt appearance, she shook her head at Silas's invitation. "I look like a m-mess."

"You look like someone who needs ice cream," Silas shrugged.

Leah chuckled, feeling her heart rate return to normal.

"Please," Silas said, placing his hand over his heart. "Let me be your friend."

Leah couldn't deny that she had been badly shaken up, and it would be nice to have someone to talk to as she recovered from her frightening ordeal. Plus, it was a bright, sunny day, and a cool treat sounded refreshing.

"L-let's go," she finally agreed.

Silas beamed as he helped her out of her buggy. The pair walked wordlessly toward his rig, giving Leah plenty of time to think.

Once she was seated in his buggy, she waited patiently while Silas went to get some water for her horse to drink while they were gone. She couldn't help but replay the shocking events in her mind. First, she'd been bullied by a group of rowdy teenagers, and when she prayed for a rescuer, the Lord had sent the most unlikely person for the job. It proved to her that the Lord was always listening and that perhaps, just maybe, she'd gotten Silas Riehl all wrong.

"Two ice cream cones, please, both mint chocolate chip," Silas said as he stepped up to the window of the small ice cream stand. He realized then that he'd forgotten to ask Leah what flavor of ice cream she'd like to have. He was partial to anything mint-flavored and decided to take a risk by ordering his favorite flavor for her as well.

As the teenage *Englisch* girl wrote down his order on a receipt pad, Silas glanced over his shoulder to check on Leah. She was still seated in the same spot he'd left her, on a bench that was shaded by several large trees that were starting to turn from green to red, orange and yellow. The picturesque surroundings made her look even lovelier than usual. Her anxious expression took nothing away from her beauty, though it worried Silas that she might still be fretting over her earlier experience with the group of troublemakers.

"Okay, two mint chocolate chip cones. Anything else?"

Silas noted Leah's grimace and her bouncing foot, a nervous habit she'd displayed since childhood, and turned back to the young employee. "Better make those cones with two scoops, and add sprinkles, please."

After he'd been handed both cones and tucked a few napkins beneath his suspenders, Silas hurried toward the bench where Leah was seated. "Enjoy," he said as he took a seat beside her, handing her one of the cones.

Leah accepted the treat and chuckled softly. "You ran over here p-pretty fast," she chuckled. She suddenly looked tired, as if that tiny laugh had worn her out.

"*Jah*, didn't want it to melt!" Silas licked the frozen treat and savored the refreshing flavor.

Leah let out a little puff of air that was even less audible than her giggle. A small but genuine smile crossed her lips as she looked down at her ice cream. "Mint chocolate chip is my f-favorite. How did y-you know?"

Silas grinned, pleased that his choice of flavor had been satisfactory. "It's my favorite too. I remembered the first time I visited your roadside stand you took a mint chocolate whoopie pie from your lunch box and gave it to me. Figured it was a favorite flavor of yours as well."

A few moments of silence passed between the pair as they enjoyed their desserts. Silas stole glances at Leah as he tried to figure out how to help her move past her earlier unpleasant encounter. It was a shame that she couldn't seem to shake negative experiences. If only he could cheer her up!

"Here," he said when he noticed Leah's ice cream starting to drip onto her hand. "Take one of these," he pulled the napkins out from beneath his suspenders and handed them to her.

She grinned a little more widely than before, making a full smile seem more within reach. "That's a clever way of c-carrying them," she replied, accepting one of the napkins.

Silas shrugged, though inwardly he was dancing with delight. A rare compliment from Leah was something to celebrate. "I didn't have enough hands to carry everything," he said.

Leah nodded as she wiped the melted ice cream from her hand. "I don't know if I w-would've come up with something so *schmart*."

She thought he was smart! Hearing Leah say two kind things about him was almost his undoing. He wanted to leap from the bench and let out a whoop of joy. Unsure of how to respond, Silas said nothing but continued to enjoy his ice cream.

Some more time passed as the pair finished their cones in silence. Leah had been staring at a large flower barrel that was bursting with colorful mums for several minutes. Perhaps she was merely enjoying the lovely scenery.

Silas began to speculate that something more serious might be bothering Leah. "Everything *oll recht*?" he asked when the corners of Leah's mouth suddenly drooped.

She gave a sigh that was low and long. Leaning forward, she placed her elbows on her knees and cradled her cheeks in her hands. "*Nee*, I f-feel *baremlich*."

Silas felt his chest tighten with concern. "Why? Did the ice cream upset your stomach?"

"*Nee*, n-not at all," Leah answered, her hazel eyes becoming suddenly shiny as if they were filling with tears. "I feel *baremlich* about how I t-treated you all of these y-years."

Silas's mouth dropped open. He was stunned by her sudden, unexpected revelation. Sure, she'd recently dropped her well-armored defenses when they interacted, but what has caused her to have such an extreme change of heart? He almost wouldn't have believed it, if it weren't for the glum expression on Leah's pretty face. It hurt him that she felt bad for having a normal reaction to the wrong he'd done her all those years ago. She hadn't intentionally done anything cruel to him, so there was no reason for her to feel bad.

"*Ach*, don't worry yourself about that," Silas

said, trying to comfort her. "It's best to leave the past behind us, *jah*?"

"I don't think I c-can," Leah admitted, "not without a-apologizing first." She turned to face Silas, her eyes intent on his. "I'm so sorry for how I've t-treated you." A gentle breeze swept by that moved the sheer white ribbons of her *kapp*, and she reached to brush them out of her face. "I sh-should've given you a second chance, especially now that we're b-both adults."

Silas was so stunned by Leah's sudden change in attitude that it took him several moments to process what she'd said. The woman who had previously been visibly repulsed by his presence now saw him in a much more positive light. Maybe the Lord had finally answered his prayer and softened Leah's heart.

"There's nothing to be sorry for. I was an ornery *bu*, and you responded how anyone would have." He hoped his response reassured her, not wanting Leah to feel guilty for something so silly.

She smiled faintly, then turned her attention back to the flower barrel.

Silas nudged Leah with the side of his arm, and when her gaze met his, he began to tell her something he never thought he would share. "Do you know why I picked on you so much when we were *kinner*?"

Leah shrugged. "My s-stutter?"

Silas leaned back against the bench and looked up toward the sky, squinting against the sunlight. "*Nee*. I was a poor scholar. No matter what lessons we were studying, I had trouble catching on. I noticed that you were *schmart*, effortlessly *schmart*. You barely had to work to get good grades, and I was downright jealous.

"One day, we had a spelling bee. Even with your stutter, which was much more severe back then, you were able to spell every word correctly. I remember how all the *kinner* cheered when you were the last speller standing. Me, on the other hand, I was the first scholar to spell a word incorrectly. On top of that, it was report card day, and you can imagine how poor my marks were. I felt stupid, to say the least."

Leah's mouth contorted. "We all learn d-differently, but that doesn't make anyone stupid."

"I didn't understand that until I was much older. My *mamm* sat me down after dinner one day and we discussed some of my lessons. We went over and over them until she found a method that clicked for me. Then every day after *schul*, we'd spend an hour or two together, and she taught me the lessons in a way that made sense to me." Silas crossed his arms over his chest. "At first, I hated having to study more, but soon my grades started improving. I was *dankbarr* for my *mamm*'s help."

Leah's face brightened. "That shows how m-much your *mamm* loves you."

Silas exhaled loudly through his nose. "*Jah*, but that's not what I focused on. I just kept thinking about how easily good grades came for you and how much harder I had to work just to earn a passing score. On top of that, I couldn't help but notice how well-liked you were by everyone. Teacher Katie and all the *kinner* loved you. You never said a harsh word to anyone, and you went out of your way to be kind. I admired those qualities you had, which also apparently came with ease. I envied your brains and demeanor, and not seeing those qualities in myself, I acted out by teasing you about your stutter." He held up his palms in the air. "*Narrish* and pointless, I now realize, but that's how my frustration with myself manifested. I apologize, again, for how much I bullied you. I hope you'll forgive me for that nonsense, but I completely understand if that's too much to ask."

Leah smiled and reached for Silas's hand. "I would like for us to try to be f-friends."

"*Jah*, that sounds *wunderbaar*," Silas happily agreed, trying to ignore the dizziness that came upon him when her cool palm rested on the top of his hand. He was ecstatic that they could finally start a friendship. A part of him worried that growing closer to Leah might one day break his heart since he was developing feelings for her that were stronger than just those of friendship.

"Now that we've worked this out, there's another matter we should settle," he said, pushing past his thoughts of a possible romance.

"Wh-what's that?" Leah suddenly looked worried.

"The pie you baked for me. Didn't you wonder why I turned it down?"

Leah's mouth drooped. "*Jah*, but there's no n-need to hash that out again."

Silas readjusted his straw hat and leaned forward. "Still, I'd like to explain myself." He paused for a moment, wondering if Leah would believe what he was about to share. "I think you're a *wunderbaar gut* baker, surely you know that."

Leah stared at him, mouth open and large eyes blinking.

"Nearly every single night, ever since I was little, my *mamm* has served a slice of pecan pie after supper. Pecan pie is my *daed*'s favorite dessert, and my *mamm* enjoys it as well. They don't seem to mind the same taste every day, but I sure do." He fidgeted, hoping he wasn't accidentally insulting his mother's baking. "After years of having the same dessert every night, I grew sick of pecan pie. Even the scent of it churns my stomach."

Leah listened to his story and chewed on her bottom lip as if she was restraining a smile. "So, it wasn't my b-baking or the fact that I was g-giving you a gift that made you so repulsed?"

Silas shook his head, grimacing and swallowing hard when the overly familiar taste of pecan pie assaulted his mind. "*Nee*, it was the pecans."

Leah let loose with a laugh that was so loud it startled Silas. He watched her as she doubled over in a fit of chuckles, hugging her sides and turning the prettiest shade of pink. He joined in her laughter, and soon the two of them were howling until neither could catch their breath.

Silas couldn't help but feel overwhelmed with joy. He and Leah were finally on good terms. If the past was truly put behind them, hopefully, their friendship would grow into something more.

Chapter Eleven

"Willow?" Toby asked in his sweet baby voice. He toddled behind Leah while she watered the planters of mums and asters that she had for sale.

"I don't know where W-Willow is, *mei lieb*," Leah answered as cheerfully as she could. "She must be around here s-somewhere." Truthfully, her concern for her missing dog had increased with each hour that passed. She hadn't seen her loyal canine since after supper last night. When she opened the door to let Willow in the house for breakfast that morning, the dog was nowhere in sight, which was unusual and worrisome.

Leah had spent the morning hours cooking and eating breakfast with her family, then preparing to open her shop for another busy day. Then there was an unexpected visit from Martha and Toby, which was a pleasant surprise.

Normally she wouldn't have minded keeping an eye on her adorable nephew, since Martha needed to go to another dental appointment. However, the added responsibility of watching the active toddler meant that she wouldn't have a single free moment to spend searching for her beloved dog.

"Want to help me w-water the *blumme*?" she asked Toby in Pennsylvania Dutch. The colorful planters that she had for sale outside the shop were popular with her customers, and she took pride in keeping them healthy and vibrant. Keeping them watered might entertain Toby, as well as keep both of their minds off worrying about Willow.

Toby reached for Leah's hand and the pair slowly walked toward the barnyard where the old-fashioned hand-pump well was located. Though their church district allowed indoor plumbing, Leah often still used the well for her outdoor water needs. Toby giggled as he held his hands beneath the stream of water, obviously enjoying the refreshing feeling. As they ambled back to the roadside stand, Leah flicked a few droplets of water from the can to Toby's cheek. She enjoyed her nephew's squeals of delight, though the happy sound didn't diminish her concern for Willow. What would she do if something had happened to her dog? Willow was her constant companion, and she knew she would be lost without the faithful animal.

When she and Toby turned the corner, Leah noticed Barbara Riehl, Silas's mother, exiting her buggy and heading toward the roadside stand. The middle-aged woman waved with a smile, and Leah returned the greeting. Leah recalled her girlhood days, wondering if Silas's parents knew just how badly he had treated her during their youth, though she didn't harbor any animosity toward Mr. and Mrs. Riehl. In fact, the Riehl adults had been kind and neighborly for as long as Leah could remember. She held back a laugh, remembering how she used to wonder if Silas had been adopted since she couldn't fathom how two nice folks had raised such a little menace.

"*Guder mariye*, Leah," Barbara said softly as she approached. "*Wie bischt?*"

For the sake of her guest, Leah decided not to declare just how anxious and melancholy Willow's disappearance had her feeling. "*Gut, denki* for a-asking," she replied as cheerfully as she could. "What can I do for y-you?"

Barbara adjusted her wire-rimmed glasses. "My *bruder* and his *fraa* are joining us for supper tonight to celebrate his birthday. I was going to serve a nice German chocolate cake for dessert, but I got distracted by a visitor and burned it to a crisp when it was baking." She chuckled with clear embarrassment. "I used the last of my sugar in that burnt cake, and I won't have time to go to the store and bake a new one before my company arrives. You wouldn't happen to have any cakes for sale, would ya?"

Leah shook her head regretfully. "I'm afraid not, but I do have s-several pies to choose from."

Barbara brightened with relief. "*Ach*, Leah, you're a lifesaver! My *bruder* will enjoy a birthday pie as much as he would a birthday cake."

The women entered the roadside stand. Leah, holding Toby's hand, walked at her nephew's slow and clumsy pace while Barbara rushed toward the large gas-powered refrigerator.

Barbara took a pecan pie out of the fridge, then turned to face Leah. "This one looks *appenditlich*! How much do I owe you?"

Leah stifled a giggle, recalling Silas's recounting of how much his parents enjoyed pecan pie. "No ch-charge," she replied, looking down at Toby who had let go of her hand and toddled over to his teddy bear that he'd left sitting against the counter.

Barbara's eyebrows rose. "That's kind of you. Are you sure I can't give you something?"

"It's yours to t-take," Leah replied, watching Toby as he plopped down on the floor to play with his bear. "With S-Silas coming around here so often, it's almost like we're all f-family now."

Leah startled herself with the tender sentiment that she'd just expressed. Referring to the Riehls, especially Silas, as her own kin was something that she'd never expected herself to say. Was it merely a slip of the tongue? She was distracted by keeping a close eye on Toby and worrying over Willow; surely her fond words hadn't been a glimpse into her true feelings. Sure, she and Silas had now agreed to be friends, and she'd seen a different side of him, but certainly, that was all there was to it.

As if blissfully unaware of Leah's inner turmoil, Barbara smiled warmly at Leah, thanked her for the pie, patted Toby on the head, and headed for the exit. Before she put her hand on the doorknob, she stopped and turned. "Are you *oll recht*, dear? You seem a little blue today."

Leah shrugged in response. It was bittersweet to feel relief about the change of subject, but once again, her mind was flooded with concern. "My *hund* seems to be m-missing," she said, unable to hide the dismal tone in her voice. "I'm awful f-fond of her and worried sick."

Barbara made a sympathetic sound. "*Ach*, I'm sorry to hear that. How long has she been missing?"

"Maybe s-since last night," Leah answered, holding back tears. "I know it isn't all that long, b-but bad things can happen to a lost *hund* in a short t-time."

"I understand," Barbara said with a wistful look. "After Silas was born, I wasn't able to have any more *kinner*, and I always felt bad that he didn't have any siblings to play with. However, we had a black Labrador. Silas said he was never lonesome with that animal following him wherever he went, so I know just how close a person can get to a special *hund*." She glanced down at the pie, then back up at Leah. "What breed is your *hund*?"

Leah explained that her dog was a Dalmatian and answered to the name Willow.

"I'll spread the word that she is missing, and I'll keep an eye out for her myself. Lord willing, she'll be back home soon."

Leah thanked Barbara for her offer to help. The women bid each other farewell, and soon Barbara was headed toward her buggy.

As she watched Mrs. Riehl depart, Leah couldn't help but realize that she felt somewhat better. She still desperately hoped for Willow's safe return, but Barbara's gentle kindness and offer to tell others of the missing dog helped to somewhat calm Leah's nerves.

Her thoughts shifted to Silas, and how he'd also had a dog that he must've been very fond of. For the first time in her life, she pitied him, thinking of how he had grown up without siblings. Even though he had a faithful canine companion, he still might have been lonely, even though he refused to admit it.

Maybe that's why he acted out so much during his youth. Leah considered this, nearly relishing this small insight into his life.

"*Kumme*, pup. I know someone who's probably very eager to see you," Silas said to the Dalmatian as they both exited his buggy. He half expected the dog to wander off toward the Fishers' barn, or maybe even make a beeline toward the house, but the animal sat patiently beside the buggy as he tied the horse's lead to the white vinyl fence near the end of the Fishers' driveway. It would have been more convenient to tie the horse at the hitching rail near the roadside stand, but since it was the middle of the night, Silas decided not to risk waking the entire Fisher household by bringing a rumbling buggy up their driveway.

On second thought, maybe I should have waited for morning to let Leah know that I found her dog, Silas thought as he held his flashlight in his mouth, aiming it just so to make sure he'd tied his horse securely. Things were going remarkably well with Leah, and he hoped that his impulsive decision to bring Willow home at this late hour wasn't a mistake. Still, he knew she loved this spotted dog very much, and knowing how anxious she easily became, he wanted to reunite the two as quickly as possible.

Silas headed across the Fishers' lawn with Willow on his heels, pointing his flashlight at the well-manicured grass in front of them. Willow let out several contented little grunts like she was glad to be home. Silas chuckled, amused at the dog's antics. He glanced toward the house, noticing that it was shrouded in slumber, except for a room on the first floor, where the warm glow of gas lamps spilled out of the windows.

Good, someone was awake.

When he quietly made his way up the porch stairs, he prepared to gently knock on the door, but it swung open before he could step up to it.

There was Leah, flushed, frazzled, and covered in splotches of flour. "Hi, S-Silas."

Silas grinned, though his face ached to release a wide smile. Flour coated Leah's black apron, hands and forearms, and there was even a spot of the white powder on her cheek. "Doing some baking at this late hour?"

Leah nodded, brushing away some of her brunette hair that had worked its way out of her bun and from beneath her navy bandana. "*Jah.* Couldn't s-sleep so I figured I'd do something useful." She glanced down at the mess on her clothing. "I got a little c-carried away." As if just realizing how late it was, her eyes grew large with wonder. "What b-brings you here?"

"I found something that belongs to you." Silas stepped aside and pointed his flashlight to the front lawn, where the beam of light landed on Willow. The dog made several small circles before plopping down, as if she could finally relax.

"*Ach du lieva!* W-Willow!" Leah exclaimed as she rushed onto the covered porch, her eyes brightening to match the light of the full moon. The dog stood and ran to her, greeting her with playful licks, jumps and tail wags. Leah dropped to her knees and embraced the dog as relief flooded her face. She glanced up at Silas, her lower lip trembling. "I can't s-say *denki* enough! Wh-where did you f-find her?"

Silas reached out to stroke the dog's head. "Earlier today my *mamm* mentioned that your *hund* was missing, so all of us were keeping an eye out for her. When I went to check on my horses before turning in for the night, I heard a *hund* barking on the other side of our barn. Sure enough, it was Willow." He laughed as the Dalmatian leaned against his leg and looked up at him with an affectionate expression. "I was gonna keep her in our barn overnight, but I thought you must be worried sick over her. I hope I didn't disturb anyone by bringing her home this late."

Leah wiped away her joyful tears. "I'm so *hallich* you did! My heart just about b-broke when I realized she was missing." She smiled up sweetly at him before rising from her kneeling position. "I can't remember ever f-feeling so relieved."

Silas had to look away from her, feeling so taken by her sweet nature and lovely hazel eyes. *"Jah,"* he chuckled in agreement. "Don't think I've ever seen you smile this much around me."

Both Leah's grin and gaze suddenly dropped, letting Silas know that his truthful words had unintentionally dulled the near sparkle of this moment.

Silas cleared his throat. "I'm glad this *hund* is now home, safe and sound." He turned and started toward the porch steps. *"Gut nacht."*

"W-wait," Leah's hushed voice stopped Silas before his boot landed on the first step.

He stopped and partially turned to face her.

Leah remained close to the house, the light from the kitchen illuminating her from behind, like a single star on a dark night. "Maybe you'd like to h-have some meadow tea b-before you go?"

Silas briefly wondered why she was offering him a refreshment at this late hour. Deciding not to mentally dissect the pleasantry, Silas stated that a drink would be nice.

Leah smiled faintly and headed back into the kitchen and Silas took a seat on the top porch step.

A few minutes later Leah emerged from the house. She padded lightly across the porch and took a seat on the step next to Silas. She handed him one of the two glasses that she'd brought outside, and the pair sat in silence for several moments as they sipped their beverages, listening to the hoot of an owl that perched in a nearby tree, hidden by both leaves and darkness.

"Isn't that a welcome sound," Silas declared, feeling more relaxed with each minute that passed. "I've always loved the owl's slow song."

"Me too," Leah replied. "I like to open my

bedroom w-window at night so I can hear them before I go to s-sleep."

"I do that too," Silas said, enjoying finding something new that they had in common. "Nature's lullaby, *jah*?"

Leah chuckled softly and agreed.

"Seems like your *hund* likes to listen to them too," he went on, pointing toward Willow. The Dalmatian's ears perked up when the owl hooted again.

"*Ach*, she c-certainly does."

As if the dog knew they were talking about her, she pranced closer to them and rested her spotted head against Leah's knee.

"I m-missed you so much," Leah spoke tenderly as she stroked the dog's head. "Don't you ever s-scare me like that again, Willow."

"I can tell how much you love this *hund*," Silas said, enjoying the sweet reunion of dog and master. "How did she get the name Willow?"

"Sh-she likes to sleep under that willow tree." Leah gestured to an enormous weeping willow near her father's barn, though it was too dark to see more than a few yards in front of them. "S-seemed like a fitting name."

"Make sense," Silas responded, taking a few quick gulps of his tea. "I had a black Lab when I was growing up. His name was Bear, and he was my best friend." He grinned, recalling the fond childhood memories. "Whenever I was in *schul* or doing my chores, my mind was always on playing with him. I used to like to pretend I was a wilderness explorer during olden times, and Bear was a wolf that I'd tamed."

"That's so s-sweet," Leah said, her voice sounding as warm as fresh-baked apple pie. "M-maybe you should get another *hund*."

"*Jah*, maybe I will someday. In the meantime, I'll be sure to enjoy Willow's company whenever I stop by." He almost added that he hoped to enjoy Leah's company more often as well but decided not to push his luck.

Willow stood and walked over to Silas, then stretched and laid down at his feet. She let out a squeaky yawn, then promptly used his foot as a pillow.

"I think she l-likes you," Leah snickered. She looked up at Silas, and their eyes met.

Though the light from the kitchen windows was minimal, and the ebony of nightfall blanketed them, Silas found himself lost in Leah's eyes.

"*Jah*, I've grown quite fond of her as well," he replied before immediately glancing away. Something about this simple, quiet moment between them moved him in a way that he'd never felt before, and the sensation startled him.

He felt Leah's gaze still resting on him, but he didn't dare look at her again, lest whatever stirrings he just felt in his heart turn him into a bumbling fool. He remained silent and reached down to rub Willow's ears, as Leah sat quietly beside him, finishing the rest of her tea.

A few more minutes passed before Leah's gentle voice interrupted the stillness of the evening. "I better go check the p-pies I have in the oven."

Silas stood at the same time she did. "I'll let you go then. You probably want to get to bed soon anyway." He handed her his empty glass, wishing to spend more time with her. "This Sunday is an off Sunday from church. Do you have any plans?"

Leah inched her way toward the door. "I just planned to do some letter wr-writing."

Though it was a somewhat chilly night, Silas felt some sweat begin to gather on the back of his neck. "I was thinking of heading over to Mascot Park on Sunday afternoon to do some fishing. Do you like to fish?"

Leah nodded. "I sure d-do."

Silas paused before he spoke again, trying to muster every ounce of courage before asking his question, certain he would be facing rejection. "Would…would you like to go with me?"

Leah hesitated. "O-okay," she finally replied. "That sounds n-nice."

Silas almost asked her to repeat her answer, fearing he'd misheard her. Sure, she hadn't enthusiastically accepted his invitation, but there was no denying that she had just agreed to an outing for the sake of spending time together. That was a good sign, a really good sign.

"Gut," he said, doing his best to shield his dopey grin. "Should I pick you up here, or would you rather we meet at the park?"

"You can p-pick me up, if that's *oll recht.*"

Another good sign.

"Sounds *gut,*" Silas agreed. "I'll be here with my buggy at three o'clock on Sunday if it suits you."

Leah bobbed her head so quickly that her bandanna came loose and fell off her head. *"Jah,* that s-sounds *gut,*" she said faintly as she bent and scooped it up in one quick motion. "S-see you then." With that, she scurried back inside and closed the door gently behind her.

Silas stood there motionless for several moments, watching as Willow plodded up the porch stairs, made several small circles, then laid down with a tired grunt. He could not believe what had just occurred. He'd asked Leah Fisher on a date, and she'd agreed to go with him.

Maybe she didn't realize I was asking to court her. Maybe she thinks I asked her to go just as a friend. Silas considered that possibility as he made his way back to his waiting horse and buggy. Truthfully, he'd be somewhat surprised if Leah didn't understand the romantic intentions behind his invitation. He had a growing attraction to her, even though that fact sometimes still shocked him. Surely Leah had also felt the spark between them tonight. Perhaps that was why she had made her exit so quickly following his invitation. More than likely, she'd also been startled by his request for her companionship, and by the sprouting chemistry between them.

Deciding not to spend time and energy trying to figure out the reason behind Leah's actions, Silas untied his horse and then climbed into his buggy. He grinned as he picked up the reins, knowing that when he went to bed and listened for the hoot of an owl from his bedroom window, Leah would also be listening for the same sound. And if he was lucky, the chorus of peaceful nighttime melodies would remind her of him.

Chapter Twelve

Should I bring an umbrella with me? Leah wondered as she gazed up at the overcast sky, hoping the rain would hold off until nightfall. She stood at the edge of her family's driveway, knowing it wasn't too late to run back to the house to grab some rain gear. In just a few minutes, Silas would be arriving in his buggy to whisk her away to the bank of Mill Creek at Mascot Park, and she didn't want a rain shower to postpone their fishing date.

Leah swallowed hard against the lump in her throat, feeling shaky and breathless. Unless she'd misinterpreted his gentle words, charming smile and invitation, she was about to go on her first date with Silas Riehl. Never, not in one million years, did she think this day would have come to fruition. She was annoyed with herself when she realized she felt somewhat giddy with anticipation. Over the past few weeks, she'd begun to see Silas in a much more favorable light. She couldn't deny that her heart started beating a little faster whenever he was nearby. She also knew that developing feelings for Silas was placing her in a situation that would prove to be stickier than the filling of a shoofly pie. It would be downright terrible to fall in love with a man who she would always struggle to trust.

Willow, who had been sitting patiently beside her, suddenly stood and perked up her ears at the sound of hooves clip-clopping on the pavement. Both Leah and the dog stared at the empty lane, waiting to see who would be coming around the bend. There came Silas around the corner, his jet-black mare pulling a spring wagon instead of the expected buggy.

As Silas drove the horse off the road and onto the small gravel patch near the Fishers' mailbox, Willow ran toward the wagon. Leah was pleased when her pet didn't bark, having feared that her well-meaning dog would startle Silas's horse.

Silas jumped down from the bench seat of the wagon. He grinned down at Willow, who placed her paws on his stomach, standing on her hind legs to greet him.

"Hiya, Willow," Silas chuckled, using both

of his hands to rub the dog's ears. "Are you going fishing with Leah and me today?"

Leah picked up her cooler and fishing pole and shyly moved toward the wagon, still feeling jittery. "I know she would be *gut* c-company, if it's *oll recht* with y-you."

"*Ach*, of course!" Silas lifted a squirming Willow into the back of the wagon with ease. "I didn't realize I'd get to spend time with two special girls today."

Leah felt her face grow warm and her gaze dropped to the ground. "I'm r-ready to go," she said, unsure of how to reply to his compliment.

"Then we shouldn't waste another minute," Silas replied. He took Leah's cooler and fishing pole and placed them into the back of the wagon beside Willow, who sniffed the air excitedly. "Let me help you up," he said to Leah, offering her his hand.

Leah's first reaction was to state that she'd been climbing into her father's wagon since she was a small child and certainly didn't need any help. Holding her tongue, she accepted his polite gesture.

Once she was seated, Silas rushed around the back of the wagon and then clambered into the driver's seat. Leah tried to hide her amusement at his obvious eagerness.

With the reins in his hand, Silas moved his

horse back onto Stumptown Road. The wagon rattled and jostled the pair as it moved from the gravel path onto the pavement, causing Leah to wince.

"Sorry 'bout that," Silas said through gritted teeth. "I was planning on bringing my buggy today, but I noticed the axle was damaged, so I brought my *daed*'s wagon instead. Hope that's okay."

Leah forced a small smile as she placed her hands on her lap, her fingers knitted together in an attempt to hide her nervous trembling.

"Everything *oll recht*?"

Leah watched the horse's shiny black mane as it bounced with each of the animal's steps. "I don't mind riding in the w-wagon. I just wish it gave us the p-privacy of a buggy." Feeling like they were on display for the whole world to see, she shrunk back against the seat.

"Are you worried about being seen together?" Silas asked, his tone suddenly shifting to match the heavy gray clouds above.

"*Nee*, it's not th-that," Leah did her best to assure him. "You know how the g-grapevine is. Folks will see us out t-together and will assume that we're a c-courting couple."

Silas's wide grin returned. "We're not a c-courting couple…yet." He glanced away from the road and gave her a wink.

Leah turned to look at the one-room school-house they were passing, the very one they'd attended as children. Hopefully, Silas wouldn't see that she was biting her lower lip to hide her growing smile.

"Anyway, it doesn't really matter what folks think," Silas went on, waving at a pair of Amish boys who were driving a pony cart in the opposite direction. "Does it?"

"*Nee*, I s-suppose not," Leah answered quietly.

Silas glanced over his shoulder at Willow, whose tail was thumping hard and fast on the wooden floorboards of the wagon. "Listen to her playing the drums. She's awful excited!"

"Sh-she is," Leah agreed, both comforted and tickled by her canine's antics. "I think she's looking f-forward to going out."

"She'll enjoy having an adventure today."

"Every day's an ad-adventure when you're a *hund*."

They both laughed at Leah's statement of the obvious while Willow continued thumping her tail and panting.

As the horse pulled the wagon down Stumptown Road, a gentle breeze drifted by, lifting Lea's *kapp* ribbons. "It feels like it's gonna r-rain." She once again wished they were riding in a buggy. "What'll we do if we get c-caught in it?"

She was about to ask if they should reschedule their outing for another time when Silas responded.

"Then we'll get wet, *jah*?" He shrugged like the idea of getting soaked in a rain shower on a crisp autumn day was the least of his worries.

Leah chuckled at his response, amused by his carefree personality, which was such a stark contrast to her own. She noticed for the first time that their differences complemented each other. Her extreme cautiousness and his breezy ways created some sort of happy medium. *It must be true, what they say*, Leah thought, smiling as Willow barked a friendly greeting at the herd of brown jersey cows that they were passing. *Opposites attract*.

Silas's cheerful voice interrupted her musings. "What's in the cooler you brought along?"

"I p-packed us a few thermoses of m-meadow tea and a couple of turkey and ch-cheese sandwiches. If you'd prefer s-something else, we can turn around and I can fix us something d-different," she stammered, suddenly feeling foolish. She should've consulted with him earlier about what he'd like to eat. What if he didn't like turkey and cheese sandwiches and she'd unknowingly excluded him from their refreshments?

Silas shot her a bewildered glance as he

brought his mare to a halt at a stop sign. "*Ach*, you're worried about that, Leah?" He quickly glanced in both directions, then clicked his tongue to get the horse moving again.

"I—I—I…"

"Turkey and cheese sandwiches sound real *gut*." He beamed at her before returning his attention to the road in front of them. "Thanksgiving supper isn't the only time that turkey tastes *appenditlich, jah*?"

The warmth of his voice made up for the lack of sunshine that afternoon, and for a time, Leah no longer worried about the gray clouds above.

"Besides," Silas continued, still holding on to his cheer, "I wasn't expecting you to bring anything to eat, so this is a downright pleasant surprise." Taking his left hand off the reins just for a moment, he reached for Leah's clasped hands. "I don't want you to ever worry about anything when you are with me."

Leah felt more butterflies in her stomach than were in a meadow full of wildflowers. Her fingers twitched beneath his hand as she debated if she should take hold of it. Goodness, she wanted to, but something deep within the darkest corner of her soul held her back. When Silas removed his hand and returned it to a firm grip on the leather ropes, she wished their innocent touch had lingered just a little longer.

As the horse pulled the spring wagon past farm after farm, each one neatly kept and sitting on gently rolling hills, neither Silas nor Leah said anything else. Leah was just fine with the amiable silence since she wasn't sure what to say after Silas's gentle touch and sweet-as-pie words.

The quiet between them also gave Leah the opportunity to mull over his observation. She did spend an awful lot of time worrying about things that might happen and what folks thought of her. Now that she considered this, she couldn't think of a single time when fretting over the future had done her any good. Was all her time spent cautiously analyzing every aspect of her life merely wasted hours? It gave her no pleasure to be so anxious, and if she was honest with herself, she'd have to admit that she was envious of Silas's untroubled personality.

The sound of water babbling peacefully soon registered in the air as Mill Creek came into view, but Leah barely noticed it. Should she ask Silas how he managed to be so carefree? As Silas drove his mare off the road, then jumped down from the wagon to tie the horse's lead to a tree, she decided to humble herself, before her former enemy and the Lord. Leah became determined to ask Silas for advice.

Mascot Park was nothing more than some shade trees, a few picnic tables, and a creek bank that led to a small dam, but to Silas, the small roadside park meant the world. It was the perfect serene spot to ponder one's life, and he wondered if Leah was doing just that.

Thankfully, the rain had held off that afternoon, but the dreary clouds still hung heavily like a wet quilt on a clothesline. Perhaps the gloomy conditions were affecting Leah's mood. She'd barely said anything since they took their seats in the grass at the edge of the water. They'd spent the past hour or so with their fishing lines in the water, and each of them had hooked a nice trout. Still, Leah seemed lost in thought. What would it take to coax her out of her shell?

"You know," Silas began, hoping that a humorous story would grab her attention, "when I was a *bu*, I'd run right home after *schul* so I could get my chores done real *schnell*. Then I'd grab my fishing pole and tackle box. Bear and I would make our way to this very spot. That *hund* followed me faithfully each time. I enjoyed his company, even when he would jump into the creek to splash and play, which scared away the fish."

He looked over at Leah to gauge her interest in his tale and was pleased to see her head tilted slightly toward his. Her eyes remained locked on the red-and-white bobber at the end of her fishing line, floating effortlessly on top of the clear, cool water.

"One day I was sitting here and gorging myself on a half dozen mint chocolate whoopie pies while I waited for a fish to bite," he went on.

Leah gasped and turned to face him. "S-six whoopie pies? All at once?"

Silas tried to control his laugh but failed. "*Jah*, six. My *mamm* had baked a batch for my birthday party later that week but being the little troublemaker I was, I hid some in my lunch pail and made off toward the creek like a bandit.

"So, here I sat on the creek bank, eating the last of the six whoopie pies when Bear brought me a stick. He was looking to play fetch, but I was too consumed with my treats to play with the *hund*. Before I knew what was happening, Bear grabbed my fishing pole and took off with it. Maybe he thought it was a big stick. I stood to grab it back from him, but I lost my balance and fell into the water. It was an Octo-

ber day, just like today, so you could imagine
that the creek wasn't all that mild."

"*Ach*, that's *b-baremlich*." Leah's voice was
coated in pity.

"I thought so too at the time, but looking
back, it's kind of funny." He snorted, trying to
hold back a laugh. "I can imagine what a sight
I was when I returned home, drenched and
teeth chattering. *Mamm* said that was *Gott*'s
way of humbling me for being so greedy and
sneaking away with so many whoopie pies."

A half-hearted giggle escaped from Leah.
"*Jah*, m-maybe so."

Silas bobbed his head and then glanced at
Willow. The happy-go-lucky dog was laying
contentedly next to Leah, her front paws dan-
gling inches above the water. The Dalmatian
was clearly enjoying this time with her favorite person.

When Leah remained silent for another few
minutes, Silas decided to gently push her to tell
him what was on her mind.

"Strange, I don't see any cats around here."
He squinted as he surveyed the creek and line
of tall oak trees that were full of bright red
leaves.

"Wh-what?"

"Well, clearly a cat got your tongue, and I
was just wondering where it came from."

Leah snickered, her smile adding to her beauty, like a new blossom on a rose arbor. "I g-guess there's something I'd like to ask you about."

"What's that?" Silas asked, so enamored with her presence that he was no longer paying any attention to his fishing line.

Leah sighed as she placed her hand on top of Willow's head, petting the dog with small, gentle strokes. "I've b-been thinking that I've wasted an awful lot of my life f-feeling troubled." The corners of her mouth drooped. "I s-spend more time worrying than anyone else I know."

Silas nodded understandingly but said nothing. He didn't want to risk that any comment from him might cause her to clam back up.

She sighed again, this time much more forcefully, as if she was very frustrated with herself. "I've been this w-way since I was a little *maedel*, since the f-first time I went to *schul*, and I've never b-been able to get over my anxiety. It feels like I spend m-most days just waiting for s-something bad to happen."

Now it was Silas's turn to frown. He placed his fishing pole on the grass beside him, not caring if he caught any more fish for the day. "Is it because of how I treated you when we were *kinner*? Are you saying you've been nervous your whole life because I picked on you so much?"

Leah gave him a look that was shrouded in sympathy. The look on her face was his answer.

"I've been w-watching how you live your life ever since th-things started going better between us," Leah admitted, the color in her cheeks suddenly intensifying to match the autumn leaves. "Now that I think about it, y-you never seem to let anything bother you for more than a few m-minutes."

Willow lazily stood, grunted and stretched, causing Leah's smile to return.

"I guess I'm w-wondering how you manage to not let anything r-ruffle your feathers," Leah said, peeking at Silas out of the corner of her eye.

He remained silent for several seconds, fearing that his initial reaction of shock would get the best of him, or worse yet, cause Leah to regret opening up. Not that Leah was a know-it-all, but he was surprised that she was asking him, of all people, for advice.

"Well now, let's see," Silas said, thinking aloud. He rubbed his clean-shaven chin. "It might sound *narrish*, coming from someone who caused such a ruckus during his youth, but I never found any reason to worry too much because of my faith."

Leah stirred at that. "F-forgive me for saying this, but I didn't know you had such s-strong faith. You joined the ch-church much later than most of *die youngie* do."

"Jah," Silas admitted, not taking any offense to her legitimate questioning. "I lived recklessly and selfishly, but deep down I always trusted *Gott* to take care of me. I'm ashamed to say I took advantage of the Lord's forgiveness in my past. I've always felt that there's no point in worrying about anything since the Almighty Creator cares for us."

Leah nodded but said nothing.

"Just look around," he went on, motioning toward the creek and trees, then up toward the sky. "The same *Gott* who created all this knows your name and cares for you. If *Gott* is powerful enough to do all that, it would be a shame not to trust Him to handle everything in our lives."

Leah's clouded expression brightened. "That's a real *gut* r-reason to trust in Him."

"I'm glad you think so," Silas said. "But we're all human, and it can be easy to forget to put all of our trust in *Gott*. When I'm having a *wiescht* day, I make a mental list of everything that I'm *dankbarr* for." He playfully nudged Leah's arm with his elbow. "One's mind has no room for worry when it's filled with thanks."

Leah sniffled, then stared into the crystal-clear water for quite some time. When she finally looked up, several tears rolled down her flushed cheeks.

"*D-denki* for sh-sharing this with me, Silas. It gives me something real *g-gut* to think about," she finally said, her soft voice trembling with emotion.

"Anytime," Silas replied. "I hope you know I'd do anything for you…uh…to help you, I mean."

He felt a flutter in his chest. Though he'd said the words quietly, he felt like he'd shouted them, having unexpectedly given Leah a glimpse into his heart. His hand started moving instinctively toward hers. Risking potential rejection, Silas held his breath as he placed his hand on top of Leah's. He was pleased when she didn't pull her hand away.

"I'm r-real glad that we decided to come here today," she whispered. She wrapped her fingers around his hand, her touch hesitant, yet intentional.

With their fingers laced together, they sat quietly on the bank, with only the music of the gently babbling brook and the songs of robins passing between them. Silas, though, could barely hear nature's melody over the beating of his own heart. The nearness of Leah and her hand so purposefully grasping his made him feel stirrings of emotions that were becoming more and more familiar.

Is now the right time to ask Leah if I can seriously court her? Silas debated this, hoping she wouldn't notice how much his palm was sweating, or just how uncharacteristically nervous he'd suddenly become. This did seem like good timing for such a proposal, considering the tender words they'd exchanged, as well as the scenic beauty that surrounded them.

While thinking on this, Silas peered at Leah and nearly choked on his breath when he saw her smiling at him, hazel eyes sparkling like sunshine on fresh-fallen snow. The inner strength she didn't realize she carried, her sweet demeanor, along with her obvious outer beauty were more than enough to capture the attention of any young man.

Silas was forced to look away from her, terrified that asking Leah to be his *aldi* would ruin the special moment they'd just shared, should she reject him. He could ask to be her beau another time. The common ground they now stood on was still very new and fresh, and he wouldn't risk putting a crack in the foundation. For now, he would just enjoy holding her hand, and maybe one day, she'd let him hold her close to his heart.

Chapter Thirteen

Leah and Fern stepped into The Bird-in-Hand Fabric Shop eager to do some shopping. The popular Amish-owned store was having a special sale, and the friends had made plans to go shopping bright and early to take advantage of the deals they were sure to find. Leah normally spent Mondays getting her baking done for the week, but she knew she would have plenty of time for that when she and Fern returned from their outing. She was glad to be able to spend time with her closest friend, especially after yesterday's outing with Silas.

After they both took a shopping cart, Leah and Fern browsed through each of the many aisles. Colorful bolts of garment fabric and quilting cottons surrounded them. A trip to the fabric store always reminded Leah of walking through a rainbow, and lately, she felt as if she were doing just that.

Fern chose several bolts of cotton fabric in various homespun prints, while Leah was drawn to the dress material. She placed bolts of mint-green, peach and periwinkle fabrics in her cart. She planned on getting enough fabric from each bolt to make one new dress in each shade, and she looked forward to sewing those dresses soon.

"You've been quiet today," Fern said as they pushed their carts toward the back of the store. "Are you feeling *oll recht*?"

"*J-jah,*" Leah stammered, guiding her cart around a sharp corner and into the last aisle. "I've got a lot on my m-mind."

"About your date with Silas?" Fern lowered her voice and wiggled her eyebrows. "I've been waiting to hear about how it went, and I'm miffed that you've made me wait this long!"

Leah put a finger to her lips and then motioned toward the other customers in the store. She didn't recognize any of the other Amish ladies, but on the chance that someone recognized her, she didn't want her business to be broadcast, at least not until she figured out her complicated emotions.

"*Ach*, no one can hear us all the way back

here," Fern objected in a more hushed voice. "Why haven't you told me how it went?"

Leah peered around a tall shelf just to make sure no one was within earshot. "I don't know. I guess I'm f-feeling *verhuddelt* about it."

Fern's smile dropped, and she lowered her voice even more. "Why's that?"

Leah shrugged, trying to downplay just how confused she felt. "It j-just didn't go how I imagined it w-would."

"What do you mean?"

Leah started to answer but the realization of what she was about to share caused her to become a stuttering mess. Feeling her face warm, she stared at the worn wooden floorboards. She took several breaths before being able to give Fern an answer.

"I'm n-not sure if it was a d-date, but we had ourselves a r-real *gut* time," Leah stammered, knowing that it was of no use to try to hide her growing smile. "M-much better than I'd expected."

"That's *wunderbaar*," Fern gasped, her shrill intake of breath causing several nearby shoppers to glance in their direction. "*Ach*, I knew you and Silas would get along if you'd just give him a chance, and I'm so glad you did!"

Leah grinned briefly at Fern's enthusiasm,

but her mouth quickly dropped into a frown once more.

"Was iss letz?" Fern asked, following closely behind Leah as they inched down the narrow aisle.

The memory of holding Silas's hand shot to the front of Leah's mind and it made her almost dizzy.

She shrugged, hoping to downplay just how befuddled she felt. "I just had a b-better time than I expected, and it s-scared me. That's all."

Fern left her cart, passed Leah, then planted herself right in Leah's path. "Do you like Silas as more than a friend?"

Leah abruptly turned to avoid Fern's playfully accusing stare. "M-maybe," she admitted as she pulled a bolt of fabric from the shelf. She pretended to be interested in the material while continuing to dodge Fern's steady gaze. "He's n-not as *wiescht* as I thought he was."

"That doesn't really answer my question."

Leah sighed as she ran her fingers over the soft fabric, noticing each one of the threads. It was easier to focus on what was right in front of her than what she wrestled with inside her heart.

"Leah?"

She pushed the fabric bolt back into place.

"I am interested in S-Silas, but nothing will ever come of it."

Fern's perky disposition simmered. "Are you saying that nothing will come of it, or you won't let anything come of it?"

Leah chose not to reply to that.

"I thought you forgave Silas for how he treated you in the past."

"I did f-forgive him, and I've come to c-care about him too." Leah closed her eyes and inhaled deeply, trying to slow her heart rate. Talking about her feelings for Silas was as exhausting as a full day of farm work. "I c-care for him, but we can't have more than f-friendship because I will never be able to fully t-trust him."

Fern wrapped one of her arms around Leah's slight shoulders. "Maybe that will change in time." She gave Leah a quick side hug, then returned to her shopping cart. "It wasn't so long ago when you said you couldn't even be friends with Silas and look how that's changed."

"M-maybe so," Leah said, forcing some cheer back into her voice, though the thought of fully trusting Silas seemed more unlikely than one of her father's pigs sprouting wings.

"Let's pray that *Gott* changes your heart," Fern went on, placing yet another bolt of quilting cotton into her already full cart. "It's clear to see that he has feelings for you. He's quite handsome too, which certainly doesn't hurt."

Leah was so startled by Fern's observation that she laughed out loud. It was true. Silas was very good-looking. His muscular build and tall frame once intimidated Leah, but now that they'd worked out their differences, she was attracted to his masculine features. His ocean-blue eyes and dashing smile certainly added to his charm. If they hadn't started off as enemies, Leah could imagine having spent many hours daydreaming about a future with Silas. She had to admit to herself that the idea of courting Silas didn't seem as outrageous as she'd expected it to be.

She shook her head to clear her mind. It was pointless, if not downright silly, to waste her time thinking about how handsome Silas was. Even if they were on friendly terms now, she knew she would never allow herself to fall for him. Without being able to trust him, it was impossible for their relationship to grow beyond anything more than a cautious friendship.

Am I turning down the chance to fall in love by protecting my heart? Leah silently questioned herself as she and Fern waited in line for their fabrics to be cut. Something about that notion felt disheartening, but then she refused to dwell on the topic any longer.

* * *

While his buggy ride customers browsed all that Leah's Countryside Cupboard had for sale, Silas walked to the Fishers' water pump to fill two buckets of water for his team of draft horses. It was a comfortable autumn day, but the animals had worked up a sweat on the journey to the Fisher Farm, and he wanted to ensure they had some time to refresh themselves. After placing a bucket of water in front of each horse, which the animals eagerly slurped down, Silas headed toward the roadside stand.

When he reached the door, he noticed a handwritten sign on some white poster board that was taped to the door. "Leah's Countryside Cupboard. Celebrating our fifth anniversary."

Silas grinned at the sign, remembering when he first heard that the roadside stand was opening all those years ago. As he stepped into the tiny shop, he surveyed his surroundings and was surprised to see that it was quiet, except for Leah, who was humming as she dusted the shelves.

"Where are all my buggy ride customers?" Silas asked as he approached her with a small wave. "Or should I say, where are our customers?"

Leah turned and offered him a welcome.

"They bought some whoopie p-pies then went to enjoy them on the picnic b-benches."

Silas noticed a nearby display of apple, pumpkin and shoofly pies, then felt his mouth start to water. "They're certainly in for a treat. Everything here looks tasty!"

"S-speaking of baked goods," Leah began as she moved toward the front of the shop, "I have s-something for you." She scurried behind the counter and bent to retrieve an item that was safely tucked away. After shuffling some things around, she reappeared with a paper bag. "I baked some extra ones in this week's b-batch since I know how m-much you like them."

Silas headed for the counter and took the bag from Leah. He opened it and was very pleased to see several mint chocolate whoopie pies covered in plastic wrap. "Wow, these look *appenditlich*! You remembered my favorite flavor."

"Well, that's always what you ch-choose when you come in for a snack." A familiar blush spread across her already pink cheeks.

"I guess I'm a creature of habit," he replied with a coy grin. Hearing his stomach rumble quite loudly, he set the bag on the counter, pulled out one of the whoopie pies, and peeled away the wrapping. "I should have one of these now, so I don't faint from hunger."

Leah chuckled at his exaggeration.

"How much do I owe you?"

"No need," she protested. "They're a g-gift." She looked up and offered him a smile that was nearly as sweet as the treats that she baked.

"*Denki* very much for thinking of me," Silas said before taking a bite of the cream-filled snack.

He nearly laughed out loud when the memory of his first time in the shop came to mind. He and Leah had been on very rocky terms, but he'd still enjoyed her baking, just as he was doing now. So much had changed in the past month or so, and Silas was incredibly thankful that they had been able to put their unfortunate past behind them.

"I noticed the sign on your door," he said after another bite of his whoopie pie. "Five years in business, congratulations! What are you going to do to celebrate?"

"*D-denki,*" Leah stammered, her cheeks turning rosy once more. "I p-probably won't do anything special. There's too m-much to keep me busy around here."

"*Ach*, you have to make time to celebrate this milestone. Every blessing from *Gott* should be celebrated."

Leah's face brightened, matching the blossoming of a flower. "I like th-that idea." Her pretty smile lit up her face, but she quickly looked away once more.

Silas ate the last of his whoopie pie and then scanned the room for a wastebasket so he could discard the wrapping. He saw a small trash can near the door, so he made his way across the shop and then tossed the rubbish in the bin. He turned to say goodbye to Leah and was surprised to see her studying him.

Like a deer caught in headlights, Leah flinched when she realized she'd been caught staring. She reached for her duster to resume her cleaning, but her quick burst of movement caused the tool to fall to the floor. She muttered something to herself as she picked it up and went back to her tidying.

Silas bit his lower lip to stifle a chuckle. Leah still seemed as nervous as a puppy during a thunderstorm, but something about her energy felt much more positive. Perhaps she was starting to have feelings for him.

He rolled his eyes at his thought. Sure, they were friends now, but that didn't mean their relationship would ever advance beyond that.

"Wh-what is it?"

"Huh?" Silas blinked several times when Leah's question interrupted his thoughts. Now he'd been the one caught staring.

"You're standing there like you need s-something else," Leah stated matter-of-factly. She pointed her duster at the gas-powered refrigerator. "Need a d-drink to wash down your snack? You can help yourself to some m-meadow tea or lemonade."

"Denki," Silas croaked. His mouth suddenly felt dry, and a cool drink would sure hit the spot. As he opened the refrigerator, he hid behind the door for a moment, debating if now was the right time to ask Leah to start seriously courting. Their relationship had improved by leaps and bounds, so hopefully, his question wouldn't come as a shock to her. Besides, he had already been sitting on this decision for long enough. It was time to put his heart on the line.

Gathering his courage, Silas took a bottle of lemonade. "I was... I was wondering..." His nerves were getting the best of him. He removed the lid from the bottle and took a long drink, buying some time to collect himself.

"Jah?" Leah asked over her shoulder, her attention still focused on dusting the shop's shelves.

Thank goodness she wasn't looking at him. It would be easier to let his vulnerability show without getting lost in her piercing hazel eyes.

"I'm awful glad that we've worked things out between us," Silas said after clearing his throat. "And I've enjoyed the time we've spent together and getting to know you."

"S-same here," Leah replied, stopping her tidying briefly to smile at him.

"It's real *gut* to hear you say that," Silas exhaled. He took his hat off and held its brim with both hands, rotating it out of nervousness. "And I'm *dankbarr* that you gave me the chance to bring my buggy rides here. If you hadn't, I might never have had the chance to see what a hardworking, generous woman you are, and how warm your heart is."

Leah spun around to face him at that remark. Her eyes were as large as the pies she had for sale, and her face was as red as strawberry jam. She looked at him as if he'd lost his mind, and Silas wasn't sure if that was a good sign or not.

"*Ach*, I'm awful long-winded." He looked up at the wooden ceiling, noticing there wasn't a single cobweb in sight. Then he dropped his gaze to the floorboards, worn but clean. He felt unable, unworthy even, to look Leah in the eye. Maybe it was a mistake to ask her to be his girl. But he'd already started his speech, and it was too late to chicken out now.

Forcing himself to meet Leah's gaze, he offered her a timid smirk. "What I'm trying to say is that I would like for us to start courting."

Leah gasped like she'd been startled by a mouse. "Y-you're asking me to be your *aldi*?"

Silas grimaced, enjoying the thought of Leah being his sweetheart girl, but pained at the anticipation of possible rejection.

"*Jah*, I want to be your beau, if you'll let me."

Leah scrutinized him like she used to study difficult arithmetic problems during their days of attending the one-room schoolhouse. "Wh-why?"

Silas stepped closer to her, taking her free hand in his. "I think you're a downright respectable, lovely woman. What sensible fellow wouldn't try to win your affections?"

"*Ach*, S-S-Silas…" Her voice trailed off as her eyes darted between him and the shop's front door. Was she worried that someone might overhear this intimate conversation, or maybe she was hoping a customer would enter and provide a distraction?

"I know you are probably still unsure of me, but I promise you, my intentions are *gut*." He guided her hand to his chest and placed her open palm over his heart. "Just give me a chance to make you happy."

No response.

"Think of me as one of the trout in Mill Creek. You reeled me in, and you can throw me back if I don't turn out to be the catch of your dreams."

Her initial scoff quickly morphed into giggles. "O-okay," she finally said, after keeping Silas on pins and needles for what felt like a month.

"Is that a yes?"

"*J-jah*, it is." She pulled her hand away from his chest, turned, and went back to her dusting as quickly as a flash of lightning.

Her three-worded response was enough to fill Silas with enough glee to send him floating up to the clouds. He fought to keep his wide smile at bay but knew he was failing to do so. Maybe, just maybe, he had a shot at winning her heart. For all he knew, he could be looking at his future wife.

"Wh-what are you smiling at?" Her amused expression dared him to say that he was tickled pink by their courtship.

"Just thinking about these whoopie pies you made for me," Silas replied as he placed his hat back on his head, hoping she would buy his explanation. "I better see if my customers are ready to leave so we can stay on schedule. See you later." With that, he shot Leah a teasing glance, snatched up the paper bag that held the rest of his whoopie pies, and headed for the back door.

Chapter Fourteen

Leah was unable to sleep that night, even though she'd been resting in bed for several hours. She lay on her right side, staring out the window, waiting for the next lightning strike to illuminate her bedroom for a fraction of a second. It wasn't the late-night storm that was preventing her from slumber. It was her own racing mind that was keeping Leah awake.

Was agreeing to court Silas the right decision? she wondered as she rose from her bed and wandered across the room. She stood at the window, listening to the rain pinging steadily against the tin eaves and questioning the choice she'd made. She'd been rattled by his invitation to be his sweetheart girl, and she hadn't stopped thinking about that moment since it had occurred.

Silas was everything she could want in a

suitor. He had a good sense of humor, he was industrious, charming and handsome. She'd discovered that he had a way of putting her at ease, and most importantly, he was committed to his faith. Yet, no matter how much Leah tried to dismiss her misgivings, doubt about his character still remained. Could she trust Silas with her heart, even though he'd nearly destroyed it in the past?

Growing weary of the constant emotional gymnastics she'd dealt with ever since Silas had reentered her life, Leah slowly dragged her palms down her face. Knowing that her mind was far too busy to rest any time soon, she donned her cozy, terrycloth robe, picked up her battery-powered lantern, and tiptoed down the stairs, being careful to avoid the ones that she knew would creak. She padded down the hall and through the kitchen, stopping briefly to watch Willow, who was asleep on the hand-woven rug in the middle of the linoleum floor. Clearly, the beloved dog was having a dream, her tail wagging and paws twitching even in her deep sleep.

Glad for the humorous distraction from her unsettling thoughts, Leah stifled a giggle as she silently exited the house and stepped onto the covered porch. She shivered at the chill in the damp night air and then turned toward the wicker rocking chairs where she planned to sit and watch the storm. She gasped and placed her hand over her heart when she noticed her father seated in one of the rockers, wearing a green shirt, black trousers, and suspenders.

"*Ach, Daed*, I didn't expect to s-see anyone out here at this hour," Leah said quietly as she crossed the porch. "Already dressed for the d-day too."

"It'll be time for morning milking in an hour or so," Ezra declared, his beard bouncing as he spoke. "Seems like the *gut* Lord wanted me to get up early today, and the cows won't be disappointed either," he chuckled after a sudden clap of thunder.

"Didn't realize it's so close to d-dawn," Leah admitted as she took a seat in the chair next to her father. His statement forced her to reflect on what had felt like an endless night, tossing and turning, and overthinking. "I'm s-surprised *Mamm* and Sarah are able to sleep through all this r-racket," she said, gesturing toward the pounding rain.

He nodded, seeming unbothered by the loss of sleep he'd experienced. "Your little *schwester* takes after *Mamm* in that respect. Both are such deep sleepers." He paused and issued another small laugh. "Willow can sleep through anything too, *jah*? I didn't realize she was in the kitchen until she let out a snore so loud that I just about jumped out of my skin."

Leah smiled, comforted by the warmth in her father's voice. "You know *Mamm* lets W-Willow sleep in the *haus* when the w-weather's acting up."

"Knowing how fond you are of that *hund*, I suspect you must wish for a lot of rainy and snowy days."

Leah couldn't deny that. She let out a little scoff, causing her father to laugh once more, though muted as if in respect for the very early morning hour.

They sat in silence for a while, enjoying the smell of cool rain against the earthy scent of autumn leaves and counting the time between lightning strikes and booms of thunder.

"Maybe it's none of my business, but a *daed* knows his *dochder*'s heart. I'm thinking it wasn't the storm that was keeping you awake tonight," her father stated, seemingly out of the blue. "Am I right about that?"

"*Jah*, I s-suppose so." She slung her long braid over her shoulder so she could more comfortably rest against the chair.

"Care to unburden yourself and share your worries with your *ault daed*?"

Though she was still unsettled, Leah couldn't help but grin. She cherished the special relationship they had. *Daed* had always been ever so kind and patient with her.

"How does s-someone know if they've made the right d-decision about something real important?" Leah asked, feeling shy when it came to speaking on matters of the heart.

"*Vell* now," her father started thoughtfully, rubbing his calloused hands together. "Ever since you were a little *maedel*, your *mamm* and I did our best to teach you right from wrong, and to follow *Gott* in all ways. Sounds like you're talking about matters that aren't so black-and-white."

Leah nodded, watching as a small white moth fluttered toward the light from her lantern. She felt as tiny and fragile as the winged critter. If it flew too close to the edge of the covered porch, it would surely meet its end in the storm. One wrong move on Leah's part and, like that little moth, she too would be headed for disaster.

"The decisions we make, especially those that are more difficult, change the course of our lives," *Daed* went on, rubbing the top of his head where his chestnut hair was starting to thin. "But even when there is no clear path to take, your heart can often find one. And with the size of your heart, my Leah, I know whatever choice you make will be the right one."

Comforted by her father's wisdom, she rose from her chair and wrapped her arms around his neck. *"Ich lieb dich, D-Daed. Denki."*

Her father returned her embrace, cradling her tenderly as if she was still a little girl. "I love you too, my *dochder*, and *Gott* loves you more. Follow Him in all ways, and then follow your heart."

After the sentimental moment passed, Ezra excused himself, returning indoors to make some coffee "as quietly as I can," he said.

Leah decided to sit on the edge of the porch instead of returning to the rocking chair, wanting to feel closer to *Gott*'s creation. She pulled her knees to her chest and wrapped her arms around her legs, hugging herself as she watched the dark, stormy night sky slowly transform into a lovely golden dawn.

Like the ground that soaked up the shower sent by the Lord, Leah willingly absorbed her father's astute insight. She prayed for *Gott*'s guidance, then examined the depth of her soul.

As the birds began whistling their morning song, Leah realized that it was her heart's desire to be courted by Silas. She couldn't deny that her feelings for him were growing. She would just have to rely on her Heavenly Father to take away the sense of mistrust that she couldn't seem to shake on her own.

* * *

"Would you like to tell me what that was about?" Ivan asked Silas as the men exited the Schrock family's barn, where the biweekly church service had been held that Sunday.

"What do you mean?" Silas responded as a strong breeze nearly lifted his black felt Sunday hat from his head.

"I noticed you weren't paying very much attention to Bishop King's sermon," Ivan said, nearly losing his own hat as well.

Silas placed his hand on top of his hat to keep it from sailing away. "I was paying attention."

"*Jah?* What was his sermon about?"

Silas paused, trying to recall what the elderly bishop had preached about during the nearly three-hour service. It was hard to recall because he had indeed been distracted. Several times his attention had drifted over to the side of the temporary meetinghouse where the women and girls were seated on backless benches. His eyes effortlessly landed on Leah, and he'd been unable to focus on anything else. He'd silently admired her as she listened intently to the sermon, his heart nearly stopping when she'd looked over at him. She offered an inconspicuous, lovely grin before returning her attention to Bishop King's sermon. Silas fought a wide grin, still in shock that a woman like Leah would agree to court him.

And yet, Leah's hesitancy to accept his courtship proposal dampened the fire of his excitement. He'd been so elated by her eventual agreement to be his *aldi* that he hadn't considered her doubtfulness until now. Would she change her mind about being his sweetheart?

"*Vell*, what was the sermon about?"

"*Ach*, I guess you caught me," Silas conceded. "But if you were spying on me, you weren't listening to the preaching either."

Ivan let out a laugh that was a little too boisterous for a church Sunday. Several nearby church members looked up from their quiet conversations. Ivan sheepishly smiled before going on in a lower voice, "So, what were you thinking about?"

Silas stared down at his white shirt and black vest, using the brim of his hat to hide his face. "I…uh… I recently asked Leah to be my *aldi*."

Ivan's eyebrows rose so high they nearly climbed off his forehead. "Is that so?" He gave a genuine smile. "I didn't know you two had gotten *that* close."

Silas shrugged. "We're certainly getting along better now, and I definitely care for her as more than a *friend*."

Ivan's smile grew even larger as he gave Silas a brotherly slap on the back. "That's *wunderbaar*, Silas!"

Silas mustered a grin, but his worries over Leah's seeming reluctance forced his lips into a frown.

"What's that *bedauerlich* face about?" Ivan asked.

Silas sighed and looked up at the cloudless sky above, squinting in the sunlight as he thought of how to best articulate his emotions. "Leah was hesitant to agree to court me, and I worry that she might change her mind without giving our relationship a chance." He let out a muffled groan as he dropped his gaze to the ground. "And if something goes wrong between us, she might not allow me to bring tourists to her place. The farm tours and stop at Leah's Countryside Cupboard have rapidly become a huge part of my business."

Ivan was quiet for a moment, and Silas could nearly see the gears turning in his head.

"Are you more concerned about your relationship with Leah or the future of your business?" Ivan finally asked, his voice more serious than a crop-killing frost.

"Both," Silas admitted. "My business is the most important thing in my life, after *Gott*, of course. I just never expected to have feelings for my business partner, especially when I don't know if she even likes me. What if I ruin my chance at making a life with a woman that I'm falling for and ruin my business in the process?"

"*Ach*, don't think like that. Leah wouldn't have agreed to be your *aldi* if she didn't have some type of feelings for you," Ivan replied, his normally animated voice taking on a comforting tone. "She may not be in *lieb* with you, but sometimes *lieb* takes time." He put his hand on Silas's shoulder and gave it a quick squeeze. "There's obviously something she likes about you, so you need to have faith in yourself, and in *Gott*."

Silas was encouraged by his friend's words and thanked Ivan for his support. They parted ways and Silas headed to collect his horse and buggy, choosing to forgo the light after-church lunch. He was determined to spend time alone with the Lord so he could pray about his relationship with Leah, their business partnership, and his own unfamiliar anxiety.

Leah decided to make a trip to the local farmer's market on the following Monday morning. The large indoor market was only a short buggy ride from her family's farm and was home to dozens of vendors, a basement gift shop, and two lunch counters where one could enjoy a tasty meal. Scents of mouth-watering fried chicken, as well as freshly baked soft pretzels, almost always permeated the air. Wandering the market was one of Leah's favorite things to do. She would buy what she needed, enjoy lunch, then head back home to get her baking done for the week.

As Leah entered the market, she decided her first stop would be at the locally grown produce stand. She purchased three small pumpkins for her pie baking. Moving on to the bulk foods stand, she purchased some cinnamon and brown sugar. Before she knew it, the large cloth tote bag she'd brought along to carry her purchases was becoming rather heavy.

Feeling thirsty, Leah decided to treat herself to a warm cup of fresh apple cider. She got in line at the snack stand and stood behind another Amish woman. The woman was holding a small child who peeked over her shoulder, and Leah immediately recognized her nephew. Toby squealed loudly and reached for her, causing the woman to turn around.

Martha smiled broadly as she recognized her sister. "Funny to run into you here," she stated as she handed her squirming toddler to Leah. "Toby and I were planning to visit you after supper tonight. I wanted to bring some jars of my blackberry jam to the road-side stand. I noticed the stock was running low last time I was there."

Leah hugged Toby close as he rested his cheek against hers. "It's a *gut* idea since I sold the last j-jar on Saturday. I could also use a f-few more jars of apple butter too."

"I'll remember to bring some when I stop by tonight," Martha replied.

"Gaul!" Toby exclaimed as he showed Leah a wooden toy horse that he held only a few inches from her face.

The two sisters laughed.

"*Jah*, I see the *gaul*," Leah replied to her nephew, still holding the boy. "Did your *mamm* buy him for you today?"

Toby bobbed his head enthusiastically and then mimicked a horse's neigh. Leah and Martha chuckled again at his antics, and Leah hugged Toby a little bit closer. She cherished her nephew and looked forward to the day when she would have a house full of her own children.

Leah turned her attention back to Martha and was surprised to see her sister eyeing her with a smirk. "Wh-what is it?"

"I've noticed that you're smiling more than you ever have before," Martha said as she stepped forward when the line moved.

Leah shrugged and took a step forward. "I'm enjoying the m-market."

"*Nee*, I mean you've brightened up a lot over the past month or so. I'm glad to see you looking so *hallich* and I'd like to know what…or who…put that smile on your face."

Leah snickered, amused by her sister's implication. "I'm j-just in a *gut* mood."

"Could it be that there is a special fellow in your life?"

Leah felt heat rush to her cheeks. Silas and his charming smile immediately came to mind. Though she could still hardly believe it, he was now her beau. She certainly viewed him as more than a friend and had decided to give their courtship a chance, but she still worried that it would be impossible for her to ever trust him completely after all the damage he'd caused to her self-esteem during their childhood. What successful romantic connection could ever come from that?

Much to her relief, Leah didn't have to answer Martha's question. It was Martha's turn to place her order, and she seemed to forget the topic of their conversation when Toby eyed a large cookie and asked his mother for it.

After both women received their drinks and Toby had his cookie, the sisters chatted for a few more minutes before parting ways.

With her cider in one hand and the handle of her tote bag in the other, Leah rounded the corner to continue her browsing and collided with someone. Some of her cider sloshed out of the cup and onto the person's salmon-colored shirt.

"*Ach mei*, I'm so s-sorry about that," she apologized, turning toward one of the nearby lunch counters. "L-let me find you a napkin."

"That's *oll recht*," the male voice replied. "We shouldn't cry over spilled milk, or spilled cider for that matter."

Leah recognized the warm voice. She spun around to see Silas grinning at her as if she hadn't just spilled half of her beverage on him. Feeling her face burn with heat for a second time that day, she grabbed several napkins and handed them to him.

"Looks like we're both doing some shopping," Silas stated as he blotted at the damp spot on his shirt. "Didn't expect to run into my *aldi* today!"

Leah nodded, still trying to overcome her embarrassment. It didn't help that her heart started racing at how affectionately he'd referred to her as his girlfriend. "I stopped to get some pie p-pumpkins. S-some animal got into our *gaarde* and ate everything but the c-cauliflower." She frowned, knowing that since it was nearing the end of the season, the little produce they had left was ruined.

"I must have something in common with that pest because I used to cause trouble and I'm not fond of cauliflower either," Silas joked as he tossed the used napkins into a nearby trash can.

Leah giggled softly at his observation, his humor making her feel more at ease. He certainly had a way of sensing when she was on edge, as well as saying the right thing to soothe her nerves.

"Would you like me to stop by this afternoon to put up a chicken-wire fence? That will keep the animals out."

"There is a f-fence around the *gaarde*, but it was damaged and my *d-daed* hasn't had a chance to fix it yet. He, *Mamm* and Sarah went to New Y-York for a few days to visit some *familye*. I only stayed behind to care for the animals and the r-roadside stand."

Silas's blue eyes showed great concern. "It would be no trouble for me to stop by and fix the fence for you. In fact, I'll be offended if you refuse my generous offer."

"Okay, *denki*." Leah smiled shyly at Silas as she agreed to accept his help. When he smiled back at her and his eyes fixed so intently on hers, she had to look away. Her breath caught in her throat, and she gasped. For the slightest moment she imagined how nice it would feel to be safely held in his strong arms, but she chased that thought from her mind. "What did you buy?" she asked, pointing to a plastic bag held in his right hand.

"*Jah*, I ordered something personalized last week over at the woodworking booth and was told it would be ready today." Silas glanced down at the bag in his hand and seemed to hesitate.

"What did y-you get?"

"Actually, this is a gift for you." Silas held the bag out to Leah. "I hope you like it."

Leah wasn't sure she'd heard him correctly, so she didn't immediately reach for the bag. When he gave it a little shake to encourage her to take it, she handed him her cup and moved the handles of her tote bag to the crook of her arm. She accepted his bag, peered inside and pulled out a wooden sign. It read "Leah's Countryside Cupboard" in letters that had been written using a wood burner. A horse and buggy were also burned into the wood, just beneath the words. The sign was quite large and had a glossy finish that shined when the light hit it.

"When you take down the poster celebrating five years of business at the roadside stand, you can hang this one up instead. A business that's so successful and such an important part of our community should have a nice sturdy sign," Silas stated, fidgeting like a nervous little bird.

Speechless, Leah studied the sign for several moments, fighting to keep her composure. Silas's thoughtful gesture moved her deeply. It took her aback to know that he would think so fondly of her little shop, enough to spend his hard-earned money on a special plaque.

"*D-d-denki*, S-S-Silas," she stammered, her emotions causing her stutter to worsen. She was on the verge of tears, and she blinked several times to keep them from spilling down her cheeks. "Th-this m-means a lot to me."

"You're welcome. I'm glad you like it," he replied. His hand rose like he was about to caress her cheek, but he quickly pulled it back.

"W-will you hang it for me when you come to f-fix the fence?"

"Of course," he answered enthusiastically, his voice rising with excitement. "I can stop by the hardware store now and then go right over to your place."

"No n-need to buy anything," Leah insisted. "You're welcome to use any of the t-tools and supplies that are in our barn."

His grin was as wide as the brim of his straw

hat. "Sounds *gut*. I'm finished with my shopping, so I'll head over there right now. Everything will probably be done by the time you get home. I'll see you later today, or within the next few days." He took the sign from her and headed for the building's nearest exit.

Leah stood motionless, watching her new beau as he walked away. It seemed that Silas pleasantly surprised her more and more with each day that passed. She watched him approach one of the market's doors, wishing she had said more to thank him for his considerate gift. Even against her formerly firm resolve, she knew their special relationship was one of a kind.

"S-Silas!" she called to catch his attention before he left the building.

He stopped and sprinted back to Leah. *"Jah?"*

Unsure of what to say but knowing she wanted to spend more time with him, Leah gestured toward the nearest lunch counter, where several Amish ladies ran a sandwich stand. "W-would you like to have lunch with me?"

Silas bobbed his head. *"Jah*, I'd love to."

As they took seats on stools at the lunch counter, Leah said a quick prayer, thanking the Lord for the wonderful morning she had at the market and for her growing friendship with her childhood bully. She wondered if she should also pray for strength not to completely fall for Silas. Hopefully, what she was feeling now was only puppy love.

Chapter Fifteen

Leah removed the third pumpkin pie from the oven and placed it beside the other two that were cooling on the counter. She stepped back and smiled, admiring how tasty each one looked.

She glanced out the nearby window and watched as Silas pushed her father's rotary lawn mower back and forth across the front yard. After he'd hung the new sign at the roadside stand and repaired the fence around the family's vegetable garden, he'd taken it upon himself to locate the mower and tend to the front yard, mowing the grass for what would probably be the last time that year. He'd been working hard and deserved a treat. She quickly located two honey-crisp apples and some of her homemade peanut butter spread to serve as a light snack.

After locating the cutting board and a knife, Leah took the first apple and began to slice it. She licked her lips as she sliced into the fruit, anticipating the sweet treat. She paused when Silas passed the window, whistling a cheerful tune as he ran the mower over one of the final strips of grass that still needed trimming.

Leah imagined that this was what life might be like if she and Silas were to marry one day. The notion of becoming Mrs. Silas Riehl didn't seem as absurd as it once did. She clicked her tongue, feeling foolish for having spent time daydreaming. It was becoming difficult to stop herself from envisioning a future with Silas beyond their courtship. The more she thought about it, the more she could see just how kind, humorous and gentle her beau was. But try as she might, she felt she may never be able to get over the grief he'd caused her in her youth and her lifelong anxiety affliction that had resulted from it.

If it wasn't for my stutter, he wouldn't have had anything to tease me about, she thought. She sighed and hung her head, once again loathing the speech problem that held her back throughout her entire life. *If I was able to speak properly and Silas had no reason to tease me back then, we might even be married by now.*

"I'm done mowing the lawn. Anything else need tending around here?"

Leah was startled by Silas's voice, not having heard him enter the kitchen. She dropped the knife she'd been holding and when she clambered to grab it, the blade sliced the skin of her palm. She gasped as she tossed the knife into the sink, then applied pressure to the wound to stop the bleeding.

"Leah! *Was iss letz?* Did you hurt yourself?" His eyes grew as large as the pies that were cooling on the counter. "Let me see," he said as he dashed to her side.

She winced as she took the pressure off the gash on her palm. "It's n-not that *wiescht*," she replied, embarrassed that she'd foolishly injured herself.

Silas grabbed a nearby roll of paper towels and tore off two sheets. He folded the sheets into a thicker, smaller square. "Squeeze this tight," he said, gently pressing the makeshift gauze into her injured palm. "Maybe I should hitch up my *gaul* and buggy and take you to the urgent care clinic in Smoketown. You might need stitches."

"*Nee*, it looks w-worse than it is," Leah argued as she made a fist around the wad of paper towels.

"You sure?" With concern deeply etched

across his face, he reached for another paper towel, then ran it under the water for a second to dampen it. "Better to get it stitched up now than put it off and risk an infection." He squeezed the excess water out of the disposable cloth, then took Leah's injured hand in his. "Are you too *naerfich* to get stitches?"

"C-certainly not." Leah shook her head as Silas removed the soiled paper towels that she'd been squeezing. "I j-just know I don't need them. It's already s-stopped bleeding."

"*Jah*, I guess you're right," Silas agreed as he held her palm closer to his face for better inspection. "And it's a *gut* thing because I would be *naerfich* on your behalf. I might faint if I had to witness someone getting stitches." He winked coyly.

As Silas used the damp paper towel to wipe away the mess on her palm, Leah felt too warm, and it certainly wasn't from the heat that the oven had generated. His touch was gentle as he held and cleaned her hand. Though she didn't understand it, she felt safe and content, even though her palm was stinging.

"Did you hear me?"

Leah glanced up at Silas, startled out of her wistful thoughts. "Wh-what?"

"I asked if you have a first aid kit." He grinned down at her, his eyes searching hers.

His knowing, closed-mouth smile reached his eyes, making their ocean-blue color brighter.

Leah's face grew so hot that her eyes started to water. Did he know she was rapidly growing fonder of him?

"There's p-peroxide and b-bandages in the r-restroom," she finally answered, hoping he hadn't noticed her stutter worsening.

Silas had been to Leah's house multiple times throughout the years, when her family hosted their district's biweekly church services, so she was certain he knew where the bathroom was.

"Take a seat over there, and Doctor Silas will fix you right up," he said before he scampered out of the room. He promptly returned with the medical supplies, leaving Leah little time to ponder about how concerned he was over her minor injury. He took the seat adjacent to her at the family's large oak table and then asked her to hold her hand out. Then he dampened the tip of a cotton swab with peroxide and applied the medicine to her injury.

"*D-denki* for h-hanging the sign, fixing our f-fence and m-mowing the lawn." Leah winced as the tip of the cotton swab touched the sore spot on her hand. The peroxide created a stinging sensation that she didn't enjoy at all.

As if he sensed her discomfort, Silas gently cradled her hand above his. "*Ach*, it's the least I could do. Is there anything else I can help out with, at least until your folks return from their trip?"

The warmth of his touch caused Leah's heart to flutter. Something was thrilling about the tenderness of this quiet moment between them.

She cleared her throat to shoo away the butterflies in her stomach before answering his question. "They'll be back t-tomorrow afternoon, s-so I'm sure I'll be *oll recht* until then."

After having allowed the peroxide to fizz, Silas once again blotted the affected area with the dry end of the cotton swab. "Are you sure? Caring for all the animals and keeping up with the roadside stand is a lot of work for one person," he said as he tore open the bandage's packaging.

"*Jah*, I'll be f-fine," Leah reluctantly responded, wishing there was a reason to ask Silas to stay. "You've already done so m-much and I'm sure you're busy with your own w-work as well."

Silas squinted in concentration as he carefully placed the bandage on Leah's palm. "Actually, I take Mondays off, except for some light bookkeeping for my business and helping my *daed* with whatever needs doing around the farm." Taking hold of her hand again, his eyes studied her palm for a moment to make sure the bandage fully covered the wound. Then he looked up at her and smiled fondly. "But everything's all caught up at home and at work, so I'm all yours."

Leah smiled back at Silas but was then disconcerted by her dreamy reaction. Surely when he said that he was "all hers," he'd meant that he was happy to lend a hand with any chores that needed doing. Though they were now a courting couple, he wouldn't truly be all hers, unless they were to marry someday.

She pulled her hand away, hoping that Silas hadn't noticed her brief lapse into senseless daydreaming.

Silas stood and walked across the kitchen, throwing the used supplies into the trash bin. "I saw a wasp's nest just above the door to the milk house. I can go knock it down before I head home."

"*Nee*, I can do that l-later," Leah objected. "Besides, we w-wouldn't want a repeat of the last time you tried to knock down a hive." As soon as the words left her lips, she wished she could grab them out of the air. How silly of her, if not rude, to bring up that incident from all those years ago!

Silas stopped and then spun around. "Are you thinking of the time I tried to knock down the wasp's nest at the *schul haus* when we were *kinner*?"

Overcome with embarrassment and unable to look him in the eye, Leah jumped up from her seat and rushed over to the counter. "*Ach*, I don't know wh-what I said." She retrieved a clean knife from the silverware drawer, still unwilling to even cast a glance in his direction.

"*Nee*, you are thinking of it," Silas insisted as he leaned against the counter. "All of us *kinner* were playing outside at recess when I noticed the nest hanging from the eaves of the roof. I took off my boot and threw it at the nest to knock it down."

Leah said nothing as she continued to slice the apples into bite-size chunks.

"That nest sure did come down, and so did all the angry wasps. They chased all of us back into the *schul haus*, and we had to stay in there for hours until the swarm moved on." He stared at her blankly. "That was what you were thinking of, ain't so?"

Leah could have kicked herself. "I'm so s-sorry for bringing that up," she apologized, mustering the courage to finally look up from her apple-slicing. "What a *baremlich* thing for me to s-say."

Silas let out a belly laugh and waved a hand through the air. "No reason to be sorry! I just haven't thought about that incident in years." Still snickering, he looked up at the ceiling and rubbed his clean-shaven chin. "I thought I was helping to knock that nasty hive down, but I certainly did more harm than good that day."

Even though Silas clearly had taken her innocent comment in stride, Leah's regret still threatened to consume her. "Such a *narrish* thing to b-bring up, especially after you d-did so much for me today. I'm ever so s-sorry!"

Silas slowly approached her with his arms held out. "*Kumme* here, my Leah."

She timidly drew near to him, surprising herself by complying with his request.

Silas wrapped Leah in a comforting embrace, resting his chin on top of her head, though being careful not to smoosh her heart-shaped *kapp*. "You didn't do anything wrong, except for worrying way too much."

Leah rested her cheek against his chest. She cherished his gentle reassurance but hoped that he couldn't feel her nervous trembling. How embarrassing that would be!

They stood there for several moments, tangled in each other's embrace. When Leah felt her heart rate return to its normal rhythm, she cleared her throat and backed away. She returned to her spot at the cutting board and resumed her task. For pity's sake, what had come over her, allowing herself to be cradled so intimately?

"I—I—I don't need anything else done around here, but you're *wilkumme* to s-stay and have a snack with me." She opened the cupboard, took down two small plates, and then glanced over her shoulder to steal a peek at her strapping beau.

"That sounds *wunderbaar gut,*" he replied, bobbing his head in agreement. "Should we have our snack on the porch so we can enjoy this *schee* day?"

Leah agreed and then said she would join him on the porch after the meadow tea had been poured and the apple slices had been plated.

"Sounds *gut*, because I'm awful *hungerich* and I might have taken a fork to one of those pies if you didn't feed me." With that, he tipped his hat playfully in her direction, then sauntered out onto the porch.

As she finished preparing the refreshments, Leah smiled so broadly that her cheeks started to ache. So far, this had been one of the best days that she'd had in a long time, and she couldn't help but notice that Silas had played a major role in it.

As Silas took a seat on one of the wicker rocking chairs on the Fishers' large, covered porch, he couldn't help but smile. A smile now seemed to be his most common expression. Things between him and Leah were going better than he could have ever expected. With things becoming so cordial, if not romantic, Silas wondered what the future might hold for their relationship. If things continued the way they were going, he could easily see himself proposing marriage to hardworking, generous and lovely Leah.

The screen door swung open with a shrill squeak, interrupting his thoughts. Leah exited the kitchen, carrying a tray with two plastic tumblers and two plates. Each plate held oodles of apple chunks, and Silas felt his mouth water at the sight of the refreshing treat.

"This is going to hit the spot," he said as he accepted one of the plates from Leah. He picked up a piece of apple and bit into it, savoring the delicious, juicy flavor.

"I'm *hallich* that y-you like it," Leah replied as she took a seat in the rocking chair next to Silas. "Apples are my f-favorite fruit."

"Mine too," Silas agreed around another bite of apple. He glanced over at Leah and noticed her dipping an apple slice into a dollop of peanut butter spread. "I never tried apples with peanut butter."

"My *grossmammi* always said that p-peanut

butter is an apple's best f-friend. Try s-some," Leah encouraged him, motioning to the peanut butter on his own plate.

Silas dipped an apple slice into the homemade peanut butter, then popped it into his mouth. "*Ach*, this is *appenditlich*. I've never enjoyed an apple more."

Leah chuckled at his reaction. "*Grossmammi* taught me lots of little tricks to make things even tastier than they n-normally are." Her mouth started to droop. "I m-miss her very much."

Silas nodded sympathetically, remembering attending her grandmother's funeral several years ago. "I'm sure you do, but you can remember all that she taught you. When you serve your tasty baked goods and other foods, her memory lives on."

Leah studied him intently as a small smile returned to her face. "That's a real *gut* w-way of thinking about it," she said, using her index finger to wipe a tear from her eye. "It m-means a lot to me. *Denki* f-for saying that."

Silas reached for Leah's hand and gave it a reassuring pat. "Of course, but no thanks are needed for simply stating a fact." He let his hand linger on top of hers for a moment, wishing that he could once again scoop her into his arms and hold her close, protecting her from anything that might ever hurt her.

"I kn-know your *mamm*'s parents, but I don't think I ever m-met your *daed*'s," she went on, interrupting his longing. "Do they live around h-here?"

Silas popped another fruit cube into his mouth. "They live over near New Holland. My *onkel* Alvin and his *familye* took over the farm about a decade ago, and of course, *Daddi* and *Mammi* moved into the attached *dawdi haus*."

"It's n-nice that they don't live too far away," Leah said, wiping her sticky fingers on her chore apron.

"*Ach, jah*. It's a long buggy ride, but a visit with them is always worth the time it took to get there. They are some of the most special folks I know, especially *Daddi*." Silas recalled what an impactful role his grandfather had on him toward the end of his wild *rumspringa*. Silas was certain that if it hadn't been for *Daddi*'s frank words and the tears in his eyes, he might have never joined the church. He might still be partaking in things he certainly shouldn't. Maybe he wouldn't even be alive today.

"Wh-what are you thinking about?" Leah tilted her head as she munched on another apple slice, her eyes resting on him for longer than they usually did.

"Just pondering the past," Silas admitted as he ate the last piece of fruit on his plate. As he enjoyed the sweet flavors, he let out a long sigh. He decided that now it was his turn to open up. After all, Leah had been plenty vulnerable with him lately. He could trust her with this sour memory.

"I'm sure you heard through the grapevine that the spring before I joined the church, I was going through a pretty free-spirited spell." He cringed, knowing this was putting it very mildly.

"*Jah*, I r-remember."

Silas took a long drink of his meadow tea, using the time to come up with a way to gently share his experience with skittish Leah while not sugar-coating it at the same time.

"I'd been friendly with a group of *Englisch* guys who were around the same age as us, and it's fair to say they weren't exactly church-going folks. We were regulars at just about every bar in Lancaster, staying out until the wee morning hours.

"I'd purchased a used pickup truck and kept it at a friend's house. *Daed* couldn't do anything about me owning a vehicle, since I was still in *rumspringa*, but he refused to let me park it at home. So, to keep the peace, I agreed that my truck wouldn't touch my family's property."

Leah nodded as she listened to his story, her mouth forming a perfectly even line. No hint of a grin, but also no sign of a frown.

Mortified by the actions of his younger self, Silas went on. "One day I woke up around noon, after sleeping off the drinks I had the previous night. *Daed* and I had very strong words with each other, to the point where I heard my *mammi* sobbing in the next room. I guess my conscience couldn't stand it, so I left and went out with my *Englisch* friends. We spent all night drinking to the point where we couldn't think straight. I was certainly not in any condition to drive a horse and buggy, let alone a truck, but I did."

Leah let out a little groan. She put a hand to her temples and rubbed small circles into her skin. Was she judging the poor choices he'd made, or maybe she was considering what terrible danger he'd put himself in by driving under the influence?

"Instead of driving my truck back to my friend's house and leaving it there, I decided I was gonna drive it home, just to get under my *daed*'s skin. But instead of following that plan through, I drove all over the countryside. I don't know if I was reconsidering that decision, or if I was so *verhuddelt* that I didn't know where I was," Silas said as his shoulders started to slump. "I drove that truck right into the oak tree that grows near the *dawdi haus* on my *onkel* Alvin's farm. I must've been going at a pretty good clip because the truck was completely destroyed."

"*Ach*, S-Silas!" Leah exclaimed, her hand flying to cover her mouth.

Silas sighed again, glad to be nearing the end of this unpleasant recollection. "*Onkel* Alvin and his *familye* were out of town visiting relatives, so only *Daddi* and *Mammi* witnessed the spectacle I made. *Mammi* wanted to hurry to the phone shanty to call an ambulance, but I wouldn't hear of it. I was unharmed but deeply regretful of the worry I caused them. I never saw *Mammi* cry until that morning, but it just about broke my heart. *Daddi* insisted that she go inside and calm down, and once she was convinced that I didn't have injuries, she complied with his request.

"The shock of the accident and seeing *Mammi* cry sobered me up real *schnell*. Once we were alone, *Daddi* gave me a talking-to, just like he did when I misbehaved during my youth." Silas bowed his head, knowing his younger self needed a good shaking up.

Leah drummed her fingers against her near-empty cup. "What did he s-say?"

Silas opened his mouth, but no words came

out. *Daddi* had been downright blunt with him about the state of his life, and the state of his soul. It certainly hadn't been easy to hear. He was ashamed of his former rowdy self, and it had been exhausting to recount the tale to Leah.

"He said exactly what I needed to hear," Silas answered her as he handed her his empty dish. "I'm ashamed that anyone felt the need to have such a talk with me."

Leah gazed at the planters that hung on the porch railing, each filled with vibrant red mums. The flowers held her attention for longer than Silas hoped. He sat on pins and needles, waiting for her feedback.

Had what he shared overwhelmed sensitive Leah? Perhaps she was rethinking their friendship, as well as their relationship, now that she knew just how reckless he'd lived before he joined the church. What sensible girl wouldn't question him? Had he made a mistake by delving this deep into his past?

Finally, Leah shared her thoughts. "I hope you don't spend a lot of time th-thinking about this, especially since the church doesn't hold a p-person accountable for their actions before they take the kneeling v-vow."

Silas was so overjoyed by her reaction that he could have jumped up from his chair and danced all the way across Lancaster County. Though she seemed more reserved than she had been during the past several weeks, she'd responded with compassion and grace. Perhaps she'd been taken aback by the story, but she didn't let her apprehension get the best of her.

In that quiet moment on the Fishers' quaint front porch, Silas knew that he wanted to ask Leah to be his bride. He'd never felt more certain of anything, even though the idea of her being his future wife might have made him laugh in the not-so-distant past. Yet, the Lord was faithful and often liked to surprise His children by working things out in the most unlikely ways.

Forming a plan to make his proposal a moment that Leah would never forget, Silas drummed his fingers, still sticky from the apple slices, on the armrest of the rocking chair.

"There's gonna be a big picnic cookout for *die youngie* at the Ebersol farm next Saturday," he said casually, watching as Willow chased a small rabbit across the Fishers' expansive lawn. "I'm thinking I just might close the buggy rides down for the day so my drivers and I can attend. You think someone could tend the roadside stand for you, so you could be my date that afternoon?"

Leah beamed at him, clearly amused by

his suggestion. "I don't think my *schwester* would mind t-taking my place for a few hours. It makes her feel awful g-grown up to be a 'shopkeeper,' as she puts it."

"*Gut*, because I wouldn't dream of going without you," Silas replied, sunshine flooding his face.

Their banter continued, but Silas had trouble giving their conversation his full attention. His plan was set in place, and if all went as he hoped it would, he and Leah would be betrothed by the end of the week. They would have a *wunderbaar gut* time at the youth picnic, and at some point, he would steal her away and ask her that most sacred question. He couldn't help but feel petrified at the thought of Leah turning him down. What an unbearable heartbreak that would be!

But with the way that she gazed at him now, ever so fondly, Silas doubted that anything would go wrong during his proposal. Lord willing.

Chapter Sixteen

The afternoon of the cookout for the local Amish youth groups had finally arrived, and Leah was thankful they'd been blessed with particularly nice weather. There was nary a cloud in the sky, and though the sun easily warmed one's skin, a crisp breeze whispered its way through the Ebersol farm, where nearly a hundred young, unmarried Amish folks lightheartedly mingled.

The Ebersol family had four sons who were all of courting age. As the picnic's hosts, they were going out of their way to make sure that all their guests had a good time. James and John, the elder two boys, each manned several charcoal grills that had been borrowed from friends and family. The younger two brothers, Elias and Saul, handed out roasting sticks and hotdogs as guests lined up around a sizable campfire.

As was customary, Leah spent the first hour or so of the event socializing with a group of her female friends. They stood near a long folding table that was draped with a red-and-white-checkered cloth and filled with more food than she'd seen since the previous year's Thanksgiving Day.

"*Ach*, there's ever so much to choose from!" Fern exclaimed as she filled her paper plate with potato salad, a handful of homemade potato chips and two oatmeal raisin cookies.

"I might just help myself to seconds and thirds," Rachel Mast, another one of Leah's friends, chimed in as she lathered sweet brown mustard on a hotdog that she'd roasted over the fire.

Leah tittered as she placed some homemade pickles onto her hamburger, enjoying the commentary. "If we eat ourselves too full, we won't be able to play v-volleyball later."

Rachel shrugged as she licked a drop of mustard off her fingertips. "I'd much rather chow down on this *appenditlich* spread and watch the *menner* play. Some real *gut* entertainment, *jah*?"

This caused an uproar of laughter from Leah and Fern.

The trio headed for the long rows of folding tables and chairs and quickly located three seats. As soon as their silent prayer ended, they dug into their meals, eagerly tackling their overflowing plates.

"Speaking of the menfolk," Fern said around a mouthful of potato salad, "I've got some news to share, if you two can keep a secret."

Both Leah and Rachel nodded in anticipation of hearing what Fern would say.

"Ivan Schrock asked if he could take me out riding tonight," she went on, biting on her lower lip as a grin washed over her face. "This will be our first date."

"*Ach*, that's *w-wunderbaar* news! You've had your eye on Ivan for q-quite some time," Leah congratulated her friend, enjoying the uncharacteristic blush on Fern's freckled cheeks. Ivan was a close friend of Silas's, and from all that Silas had shared about him, she knew Ivan would be a good match for Fern.

"Ever so exciting," Rachel gushed, making several rapid claps. "I've got my steady beau, Fern's going on a first date and Leah's gonna be hitched come the wedding season!"

Leah nearly choked on the bite she had taken from her hamburger. "Wh-what? Who said I was getting m-married?"

Fern playfully rolled her eyes. "*Kumme* on, Leah. It isn't as *narrish* as you make it sound."

"That's true," Rachel agreed, giving Leah

a few gentle nudges. Her bright brown eyes shone like new pennies at the collective girlish excitement.

Leah fiddled with one of the pickles that had fallen off of her hamburger. "S-still doesn't mean that Silas and I are g-getting married. He hasn't even m-mentioned anything about marriage."

"Maybe not, but a proposal is coming soon," Rachel confidently declared. "Mark my words."

Leah's heart jumped into her throat, making it nearly impossible to swallow. "Nee, I don't th-think so."

Rachel and Fern exchanged knowing glances.

"Wh-what?" Leah asked again, knowing that the subject of a potential engagement to Silas had not been put to rest.

"I think womenfolk can be pretty *gut* at hiding our feelings," Fern said quite matter-of-factly. "But *menner* aren't so talented in that field." She leaned across the table and lowered her voice when she spoke again. "There's *lieb* in Silas's eyes when he looks at you. If he's in *lieb* with you, he'll want to be by your side forever." Then she nonchalantly motioned toward the table where side dishes and condiments had been set out.

There was Silas, toward the end of the line

that had formed by the table, chatting animatedly with Ivan and several other young fellows.

Silas glanced in the women's direction, and he did a double-take when he spotted Leah. His smile could have stretched across the expansive Ebersol farm, and he waved at her wildly, his frenzied movement causing his hotdog to roll off his otherwise empty plate. He stooped to pick up the grass-covered hotdog before glancing back at Leah sheepishly. When she and her friends began to laugh, he did too, then tossed the hotdog into the burn barrel that had been set up for trash disposal.

"See what I mean?" Fern asked after the group's laughing fit had subsided.

Leah quietly agreed and was thankful when the topic of their conversation changed to an upcoming Sisters' Day gathering. As she munched on her picnic foods, she found herself unable to contribute much to the discussion. Her mind was still stuck on the notion of being betrothed to Silas.

Was she meant to become Mrs. Silas Riehl? In the most private, secret corner of her soul, that was something she dreamed of. The shock of harboring these strong feelings still surprised her, even though they'd been growing for a while now. She was falling in love with the boy whom she'd despised in her childhood. What an unbelievable thing to admit to herself!

But still, one naughty problem remained. Losing her appetite, Leah stared at her half-eaten meal as her friends continued their conversation. She now found herself in a spot that she'd done everything possible to avoid. She was falling for Silas, though she still couldn't fully trust him. As much as she wanted to, she couldn't force or allow herself to totally let go of the damage he had done to her during their childhood. Her mind condemned what her heart longed for, causing heavy storm clouds to rampage through her unsettled soul.

Inserting herself back into the merriment of the youth gathering, Leah pushed the troubling thoughts to the back of her mind. Surely, Silas wouldn't be ready to discuss marriage anytime soon, so she still had time to think of what her response would be should he ever pop the big question.

The youth picnic was a mighty success, providing the young Amish folks with hours of outdoor fun before the weather turned too cold. Along with the tasty food and fellowship, there had been several volleyball and corner ball games. Elias Ebersol had surprised everyone when he pushed over a wheelbarrow full of water balloons. A good-natured war had broken out as the *die youngie* all scrambled to grab as many balloons as they could carry before taking off to pelt their friends with a chilly splash.

Even now, as Silas sat beside Leah in his buggy, certain spots on his navy shirt and black trousers were still somewhat damp from where he'd been playfully attacked with water balloons. He glanced over at Leah, who was sitting surprisingly close to him. He noticed several similar damp blotches on her mint-green dress and black cape apron.

"Should I get the *gaul* moving faster so the breeze will dry us off?" he asked, half teasing and half genuine.

Leah giggled then sighed pleasantly as she looked at his mare, the horse's ebony mane and tail bouncing as she trotted down the quiet lane. "No n-need to hurry her," Leah replied softly. "The *nacht* is still awful y-young, *jah*?"

Silas agreed with Leah's input, then reminded her about the buggy blanket that was tucked under the seat, should she get cold. He was tickled that she was seemingly eager to continue their sunset joyride. Silas had never expected Leah to agree to spend so much time alone together, so each private moment still held the butterflies and excitement of their first date.

"Did y-you enjoy yourself at the picnic?" Leah asked after a noisy truck passed the carriage.

"*Jah*, very much so. Even if I did take a water balloon to the face," Silas said, laughing lightly at the memory of the incident.

Leah put her hand to her throat and frowned. "I hope you don't wake up t-tomorrow with a black eye."

"Well, maybe you shouldn't have thrown it at me," Silas jested, eagerly waiting for her response like a child waiting for Christmas morning.

Leah gasped loudly enough to cause the mare's ears to flick back toward the buggy. "I didn't throw a single b-balloon at you, Silas Riehl!" She crossed her arms over her chest and stared him down.

Silas guffawed, his laughter rising above the sound of the horse's iron shoes clip-clopping against the pavement. Removing one of his hands from the reins, he slid his free arm around Leah's shoulders. "I'm just teasing. It was Ivan who made sure my face got washed tonight. Besides, I could never be upset with you, even if you were the culprit."

Leah pursed her lips as if she was fighting a

smile. She relaxed against his arm and scooted a smidgen closer to him.

"*Gut* to know, in case I ever get my hands on another w-water balloon." Her voice broke into a giggle.

Silas grinned as he took his eyes off the road to glance at Leah, cherishing each one of her unique qualities. The sunset before them cast an amber glow against her, causing her hazel eyes to sparkle. Her lips formed a smile that was still somewhat shy as if she was hesitant to laugh at his expense. Oh, she was his precious sweetheart, and with each moment that passed, he became more anxious to invite her to spend the rest of their lives together.

Silas guided his horse to take a left on South Groffdale road, now closer to the village of Gordonville than Bird-in-Hand. As the buggy crested the peak of the hill, a spectacular view of fertile Lancaster County farmland came into sight. White and red barns dotted the landscape like freckles. Fall foliage in a vast variety of colors decorated the small spaces between fields that stood barren after the harvest. The sunset, turning from orange to pink, then pink to purple, shaded the countryside in a most breathtaking rainbow of natural colors.

Leah placed her hand over her heart. "Wh-what a *wunderbaar schee* sight!"

Silas checked the buggy's mirrors to make sure no cars were approaching them from behind as he brought the horse to a halt. Wrapping one of his arms around Leah for a second time, he beheld the scenic view with her, deciding this would be the moment that would forever change their lives.

"It's like *Gott* planned this sunset just for us, ain't so?"

Leah nodded her agreement, then rested her head against his shoulder.

"There's nothing in this world more *schee* than a sunset, except for you. You know how much I've come to care for you, don't you?"

She lifted her head, perked up by his sudden loving sentiment. "I c-care for you too, Silas."

He placed his hand gently against her cheek, letting it linger there for a moment. "*Ich lieb dich*, Leah." He leaned closer to her, so close that their noses nearly touched. Putting his hand beneath her chin, he tilted her face upward so her lips could meet his. "*Ich lieb dich*, and I know I always have."

He closed his eyes and leaned toward her, anticipating the sweetness of their first kiss. Instead, he felt Leah suddenly pull away, the warmth of her breath no longer against his cheek.

Silas opened his eyes and was taken aback

to see Leah shrunken back in her seat, staring at him with wide eyes. She looked thoroughly startled as if spooked by a sudden thunderclap on a cloudless day.

It took Silas several moments to process what had just occurred. They stared at each other, both stunned into silence, though for obviously different reasons. He had just confessed his most intimate feelings, his love for her, and she'd rejected him. As the sun sunk into the horizon, they continued to sit there, staring at each other without speaking.

"You...you still don't trust me, do you?" Silas asked, his voice low and heavy with shock and heartbreak. It had dawned on him that Leah's hesitation to accept his love was a deep-seated issue, one that he thought they'd overcome quite some time ago. He might as well have fallen in love with the old stone wall on his father's farm.

"*Nee*, it's n-not th-that," Leah swiftly responded, stumbling over her words like a toddler who was learning how to walk.

Silas wasn't buying it. He saw the look of wariness she wore, though she must've been doing her best to try to conceal it. "That's it, isn't it? After all that we've been through, after how much I've done to show you how sincere I am, you still don't trust me."

"S-S-Silas," she stammered, reaching for his hand, her eyes growing shiny with unshed tears. "S-surely, you can u-understand that—"

"It doesn't matter," he huffed as he pulled his hand away from her grasp.

Now with both hands on the reins, he gave the lead a good slap. His horse issued an annoyed whinny. She started forward quickly, which caused the buggy to lurch.

"Whatever I say, whatever I do, it will never be enough," he grumbled, more to himself than to Leah.

"It's n-not a m-matter of being enough."

"*Jah*, it is, because you need everything to be perfect," he shot back. The harshness in his voice tasted unfamiliar, yet it wasn't as bitter as the grief of heartbreak that burned in his chest.

He whistled to the horse to get her moving faster, guiding her to make a left onto Musser School Road. This move started their ride back to Bird-in-Hand. It was better to get Leah home as soon as possible, now that the evening had been ruined.

"It's not th-that I need everything to be p-perfect," Leah protested, her meek voice rising as she scooted away from Silas. "I'm s-surprised that y-you can't be more p-patient with me." She crossed her arms and looked away from him. "Especially since y-you're the one who wr-wronged me."

Silas scoffed as he flicked on the buggy's battery-powered headlights. "*Jah*, I did treat you badly when we were younger. But in case you haven't noticed, it's been almost a decade since then. It's clear to see that you are never going to let me forget the past." He fought to keep his voice at an even tone, feeling his right eye twitch with frustration.

Leah's head spun around to face him. "T-treat me badly? You were d-downright *baremlich*, S-Silas! The way you treated me ch-changed my whole l-life!" She wiped away a single tear before it could roll down her cheek. "It's your f-fault that I'm always a *naerfich* wr-wreck!"

Silas set his jaw firmly, staring into the dark road in front of them. "There's no sense in me apologizing, yet again, for something that I can't change. I cannot change how I acted during my childhood, Leah. My apologies have clearly fallen on deaf ears, anyway."

Leah began to sniffle. She pulled a dainty handkerchief out of her dress sleeve and dabbed at her eyes and nose. "I knew this was a m-mistake. I knew you w-wouldn't understand."

Silas didn't know what hurt worse: seeing

his beloved weep, hearing her admit her distrust of him or the fact that he loved a woman who would never love him in return.

"If I'm so *wiescht*, we probably shouldn't be courting," he muttered, unsure if Leah had heard him over her sobs.

"M-maybe we shouldn't be."

Silas had made the remark out of boiling frustration but hadn't truly meant for them to break up. Hearing how readily Leah agreed to the notion made him nearly sick to his stomach. He'd lost his darling girl.

Maybe she'd never been his in the first place.

Neither one of them said a single word for the half-hour ride back to the Fisher farm. Leah's continuous sniffling created a melancholy melody as Silas brought the carriage to a halt at the edge of the Fishers' long driveway. Leah hopped out of the buggy and darted toward the house without giving Silas a second glance.

Silas let the horse slowly walk back home, feeling dejected and lonelier than he'd ever thought possible. He'd been stupid to think Leah would have ever given their relationship a chance after its rocky beginnings. Earlier today he'd thought they'd part ways that evening as a newly betrothed couple. Now it seemed like their relationship was over.

The wounds were too fresh and the hour too

late for Silas to attempt mending the rift between them. Hanging his head, he opened his heart a second time that night, but this time he spoke to his Heavenly Father.

Lord, please make a way for Leah to see just how much I love her. Without Your intervention, I fear our relationship will never be healed.

Chapter Seventeen

Silas allowed a few days to pass before deciding to visit Leah in hopes of repairing their relationship. That weekend had included an off-Sunday in their church district, so there wasn't the opportunity to steal her away for a few moments following the service. When customers at Riehl's Buggy Rides requested the "Amish Farm and Shop Tour," he'd sent Ivan or one of his other buggy drivers over to the Fishers' place. He figured he'd give Leah ample time to cool off from their heated exchange. He also needed time to collect his thoughts.

It was nearly six o'clock that Saturday night when Silas hopped down from his rig. He glanced at Leah's Countryside Cupboard as he tied his horse to the hitching rail at the edge of the small parking lot. The Closed sign was hung on the door, as he'd expected to see, but the shop's windows were wide-open, and Leah could be heard humming a sorrowful melody as she moved about the shop.

She sounds sad because of me, Silas thought, feeling chock-full of apprehension. *Hopefully, she'll be willing to have a conversation with me instead of another bickering match. Maybe she's even missed me as much as I have missed her.*

Willow paced around in front of the shop, her nose to the ground, picking up the scent of all the customers who had visited that day. She soon lifted her head and pranced over to Silas, tongue lolling and tail wagging as if she was smiling at him.

"At least someone's happy to see me," Silas said to the dog, brightening somewhat as he scratched her spotted head. Spending a few minutes petting the animal allowed him some time to build up his courage, which was greatly needed. He took a few deep breaths, knowing this might be his one and only chance to work things out with Leah. This could very well be the most difficult challenge of his life. Still, Leah Fisher was worth the fight.

When Silas entered the shop, he flinched at the light ringing of the bell that hung above the door, his nerves on edge.

Leah stood near a rack of postcards that featured countryside scenes, restocking the slots that looked somewhat sparse. Her eyes darted toward the door, and she let out a little gasp.

"Got any mint chocolate whoopie pies?" Silas asked, overcome with awkwardness and unsure of how to break the thick ice.

Leah frowned. "Over on the c-counter. Help yourself."

"Denki." Silas gave her a crooked smile and then headed for the counter. He selected a whoopie pie, which he would need to save for later. He couldn't handle its rich sweetness now, not when his stomach was doing somersaults. He stood in place, debating if he should approach Leah or give her ample pace.

"Haven't seen you since the day of the *die youngie*'s picnic," he went on, cringing at the squeak in his voice. He cleared his throat and pressed on. "How's business been here?"

Leah looked up from the box of postcards she had balanced on her hip, her glower as sharp as a hunting eagle's glare. "Really? That's what you came h-here to ask?"

Silas fidgeted with the brim of his straw hat. "That and the whoopie pie."

When Leah's stony expression didn't crack a smile, he knew this conversation was going to be even more difficult, and important, than he'd originally anticipated.

Knowing that their potentially blissful future was on the line, Silas mustered a cautious grin. He moved across the shop slowly, hoping the creaking floorboards wouldn't irritate her more.

"I'm awful sorry about that argument we had. I'm embarrassed about how I acted," he confessed with the utmost sincerity. "I shouldn't have spoken to you so harshly."

Leah said nothing and continued to stock postcards, though the color in her cheeks greatly intensified.

Maybe it was a good thing that she wouldn't make eye contact with him. One glimpse into Leah's expressive eyes would be his undoing.

"When I shared about how hard I've fallen for you, I'd hope you'd say that you had the same feelings for me," Silas continued, nearly choking on his words. "When you didn't, I reacted like a spoiled *kind*. I'm sorry for raising my voice and speaking unkindly."

Leah finally looked up from her work, her eyes appearing shinier than they usually did. "I unders-s-stand," she stammered as the corners of her mouth drooped. She spun the rack of postcards, making sure each slot had been adequately filled, apparently doing anything to avoid Silas's fixed, pleading gaze.

He stepped a little closer, feeling the

whoopie pie begin to squish in his hand as his grip on it intensified. "Do you think things can go back to the way they were?"

Leah dropped the box of extra postcards to the floor and spun toward the door. "I n-need to go water the *b-blumme* that are for sale," she replied as the box landed with a light thud.

When she moved to brush past him Silas darted to the side, blocking her path. "Won't you please talk to me? Can we try to move past this ugly thing that's come between us?"

Leah hung her head, staring down at the shop's dust-free floor. "I'd r-rather you not b-bring your buggy r-rides here anymore."

Silas frowned so severely that his face ached. Stopping the farm tours would certainly cause a negative effect on his business, though right now, that felt like the least of his worries.

"That's not what I'm asking about," he stated, noticing a dull pain in his chest when Leah's chin started to tremble.

She looked up at him, several tears rolling down her cheeks like raindrops racing down a windowpane. "Wh-what exactly are you a-asking me?"

Silas inched even closer, so close now that he could wrap her petite frame in a loving, protective embrace. "I think you know," he whispered, using his thumb to gently wipe away her tears.

Leah sighed heavily, standing motionless. She finally looked up at him and grimaced. "I'm s-so sorry, S-Silas. I should've never agreed to a c-courtship."

Silas felt his heart drop to the pit of his stomach. "Why? What's changed?"

"It's what hasn't ch-changed," Leah sobbed, covering her face with her hands as a fresh round of tears dampened her cheeks. "It's my f-fault. I just c-can't let go of—"

"I get it," Silas interrupted her, having no desire to hear the end of that sentence.

"I'm s-sorry," she said tearfully.

Silas felt his heart crumble into pieces. He didn't know who he pitied more; himself, for having self-sabotaged his relationship with his future sweetheart during his oblivious boyhood days, or Leah, for choosing to cling to pain instead of releasing it in exchange for the sincerest love a person could experience.

"I hate m-myself for not being able to move f-forward," Leah gasped, her cheeks and the tip of her nose now red.

Unable to stand the sight of her feeling so grim, Silas pulled Leah into his arms and held her close to his heart as she cried, his soul grieving alongside hers.

"*Ach*, Leah. If you only knew how very

much you are loved, there'd be no room for any *wiescht* feelings like that."

She allowed him to cradle her for several moments, the two of them embracing together in the privacy of the closed shop. Silas felt his eyes start to flood, knowing that this would be the last time he'd ever have the chance to hold the only woman he had ever loved. He blinked rapidly to keep his tears at bay, refusing to fall apart in front of Leah.

Leah was the first one to pull away. "I'm s-sorry to have w-wasted your time," she said softly after her tears had subsided.

"I'm not sorry," Silas replied with a small, pained grin. "I would never consider the time we spent together as wasted."

Leah took several quick steps back, like a cat who just had her tail accidentally stepped on. "I've g-got to go w-water the *blumme*." She wrung her hands together so tightly that her knuckles loudly cracked. "N-no one will buy w-wilted *blumme*."

Realizing that Leah was trying to excuse herself instead of enduring a lengthy goodbye, Silas nodded and shoved his trembling hands into his pockets. "I'll let you get back to work." He turned and plodded toward the exit, feeling as if he'd just fallen into an old, murky, sludge-filled well.

"Leah," he started again as he stood near the door, his hand on the brass doorknob. "This doesn't mean that I've stopped loving you." His heartfelt words surprised him as they left his lips. Such a tender thing to admit, especially after facing rejection.

Leah inhaled sharply and started shaking like a field mouse that had been spotted by a hawk. She spun to face away from him, perhaps unable to bear the sight of him any longer.

She was refusing to acknowledge him at that point, which stung nearly as much as her initial dismissal of his affections. If this was to be the last time they ever had a moment to speak privately, Silas wasn't going to leave a single word unsaid.

"*Ich lieb dich,* Leah. I always will. I'll never give up hope that you'll change your mind about us."

Without waiting for a response that he was certain would never come, Silas opened the door and exited the shop, wincing again at the cheerful jingle of the shop's little bell as he passed beneath it.

Silas hurried across the small parking lot, making a beeline toward his waiting horse and buggy. He moved so quickly that he nearly slid on the gravel beneath his work boots. He hoisted himself into the rig, desperately needing a few moments of privacy before taking the time to untie his mare's lead from the hitching rail.

Once settled into the driver's seat, he closed his eyes tightly and pinched the bridge of his nose, exhaling slowly through pursed lips to keep himself from having an emotional breakdown. To say that this rendezvous hadn't gone as he'd hoped was a colossal understatement.

Leaning forward in his seat, Silas placed his elbows on his knees and cradled his head in his hands. He poured out his soul to the Lord, desperately petitioning his Heavenly Father to soften Leah's heart on his behalf. It would take a heaven-sent miracle to do so.

A little over a week had passed since Leah excommunicated Silas from her life, and though it was something that she knew needed to be done, she still felt miserable. Any young lady might have been tickled pink when the man she'd fallen for confessed his mutual feelings, but sadly, she hadn't been blessed with that experience.

When Silas had leaned in to kiss her on the evening of the picnic, Leah's heart had nearly stopped, partly from the thrill of new love, and partly because she couldn't allow herself to surrender to his kiss. How could she and Silas ever have a future together when she couldn't move her mind out of the past? The chains of fear and pain still had her imprisoned, no matter how strongly she tried to shake herself free. Rather than allow her already deep love for Silas to grow, she'd decided to pull away from him, putting an abrupt halt to their communication.

Did I make the right decision? Leah wondered as she climbed into her buggy. She picked up the reins and guided Jolly, her family's most agile driving horse, onto the road. After completing all of her baking earlier that Monday morning, she hoped a change of scenery would improve her spirits, or at least force her to think of anything other than Silas.

Rather than going to her usual favorite stores in Bird-in-Hand and nearby Intercourse, she made a last-minute decision to journey to the New Holland area, where a combination dry goods and hardware store had recently opened. She was determined to get there despite her near-constant gloom, and the fact that Jolly was acting more headstrong than usual.

After a very lengthy buggy ride, Eby's Variety Store came into sight, and Leah started to perk up. Maybe she would get a good deal on some new cookware, or perhaps she would find a pretty new handkerchief. Except for a single car and one other buggy, the parking lot was empty, meaning she would enjoy the pleasure of having most of the store to herself.

Just as she turned Jolly into the parking lot, a very large dog stuck its head out the parked car's window and let out several loud woofs. Jolly threw her head back and let loose with a shrill neigh. The touchy mare stamped her hooves and darted sharply away from the barking dog, causing the buggy to jostle around.

"Wh-whoa!" Leah exclaimed as she tugged on the reins, trying to regain control of the horse. "It's *oll recht*, J-Jolly!" She'd had plenty of experience with stubborn ponies and even the enormous Clydesdales that her father used to pull his farm equipment. But no matter how gently she spoke to the mare, or how much strength she used when pulling on the reins, Jolly would not be soothed. The horse frantically whinnied and stomped her front legs, grunting and lurching the carriage around enough to slide Leah across the buggy's bench seat.

Gritting her teeth, Leah fought for control. After several frightening moments, she was able to settle Jolly enough to lead her to the hitching rail.

Leah hopped out of the buggy and tied the lead to the hitching post. She made sure the knot she tied was tight in case Jolly spooked again. Once the horse was secured, she let out a sigh of relief and wiped away the perspiration that had formed between her eyebrows.

She reached into the buggy for her plain black purse, and once it was slung over her shoulder, she turned toward the shop. Just as her gaze landed on the store's entrance, the door swung open, and out came Silas with a plastic shopping bag in his hand.

Leah froze beside the back wheels of her buggy hoping she hadn't been spotted, but it was too late. Silas was waving, and that was more than her heart could bear. Without acknowledging his greeting, she spun around and darted back to the hitching rail to untie Jolly's lead, deciding she could visit Eby's Variety Store some other time.

"Leah!" Silas called as he sprinted to catch up with her, his boots pounding across the pavement. *"Wie ghets?"*

Leah ignored Silas's greeting. She undid the knot she'd made in the leather ropes, then scrambled back into the privacy of her buggy.

"Aw, you don't have to hide," Silas cooed as he approached her buggy, his head tilted to the side. "Ain't like we're *kinner* playing hide and seek at the *schul haus* anymore."

Leah swallowed the bile that was rising in her throat. "We n-never played hide and seek."

Silas grimaced. "I'm only teasing." He stepped a little closer, nearly leaning into her buggy. "Did you come to check out the new store? It's mighty nice inside." He held up the plastic bag. "Got my *grossmammi* a real nice leather journal for her birthday."

Leah chewed on her tongue, hoping the uncomfortable sensation would keep her pressing tears at bay. "Y-you know," she said as she stared at Jolly's swishing tail and flicking ears, "I don't really feel like m-making small talk."

"*Jah*, it's kind of awkward," Silas agreed. "Would you like to go somewhere where we can talk more openly?"

What I want is to erase the past so that I could freely give my heart to you, Silas Riehl. The thought made Leah even more heartsick, and she was suddenly overwhelmingly numb.

"Leah?"

"*Nee*, I'm g-going home." Feeling the all-too-familiar tears starting to well in her eyes, she began to back up her horse.

Jolly issued several annoyed grunts while tossing her mane. She threw her head in the air and swung it forcefully from side to side as if trying to shake off her bridle.

"Your *gaul* seems upset. Maybe you should

wait until she calms down," Silas pointed out, concern growing across his face as he watched the mare's unnerving antics.

"I n-need to go home," Leah repeated, glancing in the rearview mirror to make sure the coast was clear for a hasty exit.

"Listen, I understand if you don't want to talk to me, but you should let your *gaul* relax before taking her out on the road. Why not take your time browsing around the store? By the time you're done, she should be calmed down."

Becoming more annoyed by the minute, Leah shot Silas a glare that could freeze over Mill Creek. "I can h-handle my *gaul*. I d-don't need you telling me wh-what to do," she snapped at him.

Silas stared back at her and straightened his posture. "I work with *geilsfleesch* all day, and I have for years. I'm telling you that this one isn't safe to have out on the road right now."

As if agreeing, Jolly squealed loudly, pinning her ears back and stomping.

Silas gestured toward the mare. "See? She's spooked over something."

"I d-don't know who you think you are, but you have no r-right to b-boss me around," Leah said, raising her voice to make sure she was heard over Jolly's neigh that sounded more like a roar. She felt heat rising up her neck and spreading to her cheeks, her frustration fueling her stutter.

Silas scoffed and stared up at the sky as if asking the Lord for strength. "I'm someone who loves you, Leah. I have every right to keep you out of harm's way, especially when you're too stubborn to do it yourself."

"S-stubborn?" Leah shouted as she felt her blood start to boil.

At the same time, the ear-splitting sound of a motorcycle pierced the air as the bike whizzed by. Jolly bared her teeth at the unbearable sound, her grumbly neighing morphing into a squeal. She took several rapid steps forward, zig-zagging and whipping around the buggy in her unsteady path.

What happened next lasted only a few seconds, but to Leah, time stood still. Fighting for control over the wild horse with all her might, she managed to set the buggy's brake. The hairs on the back of her neck stood up at the uncomfortable sound of the buggy's iron wheels scraping across the blacktop as Jolly urged forward.

"*Ach*, J-Jolly, please don't d-do this!" Leah cried over the horse's frightened screams, fearing that she, someone else or her horse might soon be hurt. "*Gott*, p-please help me," she prayed aloud, her rapid heartbeat feeling stuck in her throat.

Jolly suddenly stopped pulling the nearly immovable buggy, only to suddenly rear up into the air. Her front legs kicked wildly then crashed back down to the pavement before using her back legs to try to kick at the buggy.

As Leah feared for her life, a sudden force wrapped around her and firmly whisked her out of the driver's side of the buggy. In one swift move, Silas had pulled her out of the buggy and a safe distance away from Jolly's perilous behavior. They both landed with a thud against the pavement, giving them both several scrapes and bruises.

"Get back," Silas urged Leah once they had scrambled to their feet.

Leah watched in horror as Silas raced back toward danger. He managed to swipe the reins out of the buggy and wrap them tightly in his fist. He approached the irate horse, speaking to her in a firm yet calm voice as he ran his free hand along the animal's side. The horse reared again just as Silas appeared in front of her. One of her hooves clipped Silas in the chest when he got too close for comfort. He fell to the ground and landed on his back, just beneath the out-of-control mare.

"Silas! L-look out!" The yell ripped from

Leah's throat so intensely that it stung, but she barely felt the pain in the midst of her distress. If anything happened to Silas, she would never forgive herself for bringing Jolly out that day. "Protect him, *Gott*," she begged the Lord out loud, nearly at the point of hyperventilation.

Silas rolled out of the way mere seconds before Jolly's hooves made sharp contact with the ground. He sprang up as if he hadn't just been nearly killed by the beast, holding his hand high in the air in front of the animal, shushing her with assertiveness. When Jolly snorted several times and became a bit more still, Silas grabbed her bridle, keeping her from throwing her head around anymore. Several painfully long moments passed as he continued to talk to the horse, stroking her nuzzle until she stood completely still. He then led her back to the hitching rail, dragging the buggy behind her, the locked wheels leaving scratches on the pavement.

When Silas sprinted back to Leah, she immediately collapsed into his protective embrace.

"I th-thought you were g-going to be k-killed," Leah sobbed, resting her cheek against his chest. Her tears mixed with the dirt from Jolly's hoof that had been left on his shirt. "I've n-never been so s-scared!" She continued to shake and weep as she clung tightly to her former beau. She became overwhelmed with thankfulness to feel the warmth of his skin beneath her touch.

"It was nothing any farmer's son hasn't dealt with before," Silas replied, perhaps minimizing the ordeal for Leah's sake. "Are you hurt?"

Still unable to calm herself, Leah shook her head. "I'm f-fine." She stepped back and covered her mouth with her raw palms, gasping when she noticed a large rip and a few small drops of blood on Silas's blue shirt. *"Ach, nee!"*

Silas glanced down at his damaged, soiled shirt and shrugged. "Just a little nick from her horseshoe." He gave her a reassuring smile. "It'll take a lot more than a little scrape to ruin my day."

His lighthearted comment helped Leah's sobbing to cease, but her rapid breathing and trembling continued. "I can't b-believe you risked your l-life like that," Leah said, her voice fluttering like the last leaf on a maple tree during a strong autumn gust.

Silas grinned down at her, his eyes becoming lost in hers. "I wasn't going to let anything happen to you. Someone had to teach your *gaul* not to mess with Leah Fisher."

Leah choked on a chuckle and then wiped

her face when middle-aged Jacob Eby opened the shop's door and stepped outside.

"Need any help? I thought I heard a ruckus," Jacob asked, the slight breeze rustling his long, wiry beard.

Silas explained what had occurred, then assured Jacob that everything was under control. When Jacob headed back into the store, Silas returned his attention to Leah.

"My *Groosseldre* live only a short drive from here. Let me take you to their *dawdi haus*. You can rest there, and I'll come back on foot for your *gaul* and buggy."

"I don't want to c-cause any more *druwwel* than I already h-have," Leah said after several sniffles, declining his offer. "I'll j-just take my time sh-shopping, and Jolly should be p-plenty settled by the time I'm done."

Silas wrapped both of his hands around one of hers. "It's no trouble at all. Besides, I was headed over to see my *Groosseldre* anyway to give *Mammi* her birthday gift." Letting go of her hand, he retrieved the shopping bag that he'd dropped during his rescue mission.

Leah smiled, finally catching her breath. The prospect of meeting his paternal grandparents was appealing. She was particularly interested in his grandfather, whom she recalled had played a major part in setting Silas on the straight and narrow path. Though she was shaken up and certainly not looking her best, something within her, perhaps a voice that wasn't even her own, compelled her to accept Silas's suggestion.

As the pair gingerly entered his buggy, Silas chatted about his grandfather's job as a harness maker, and his grandmother's "world famous shoo-fly pies," though Leah had trouble giving their conversation her full attention. How could she, when Silas had so bravely and selflessly protected her when she needed him most?

The boy who I once thought ruined my life has just saved it, she mused, questioning her decision to break off their courtship. *Is it possible that the Lord allowed this ordeal to happen to show me that Silas can be trusted?*

Chapter Eighteen

"Ach, I'm s-such a mess. I'm going to make a *wiescht* first im-impression," Leah said after taking a deep breath. She and Silas walked across an immaculately maintained lawn that led to the large white farmhouse, and a smaller attached *dawdi haus* where Silas's grandparents lived.

"Well, you're certainly the most *schee* mess I've ever seen," Silas replied as he gave her a charming wink.

Leah blushed at the compliment. She wrung her hands together, forgetting about the brush burns on her palms. "I don't know why I'm f-feeling so *naerfich*."

"You went through a lot today," Silas replied as they approached the corner of the *dawdi haus*. "But my *Groosseldre* are real nice folks, and they'd be glad to meet you even if you weren't so *schee*."

Leah couldn't help but smile at that.

An elderly Amish man wearing a lilac shirt, black trousers and suspenders, and a gray beard that nearly touched his stomach came into sight as they rounded the corner. Hearing the pair approaching, he looked up and leaned on his hoe, not moving from where he stood in the small vegetable garden.

Silas waved a greeting. *"Wie bischt, Daadi?"*

The old man's wrinkled expression warmed at the sight of his grandson. "Doing well, but I can't say the same for all the weeds I just tore up. They're still putting up a fight, even though the first frost can't be too long away." He grinned as he turned his attention to Leah. "Who's your friend?"

"This is Leah Fisher," Silas said as he motioned to her. "Leah, this is my *daed*'s *daed*, Samuel Riehl."

Samuel's mouth hung open. His thick eyebrows rose on his forehead and disappeared beneath the brim of his straw hat. "Leah Fisher, did ya say?" He extended a callused hand to her. "I never forgot that name. I've been waiting years to meet you."

Leah shook hands with Samuel, wondering why he knew her name and wanted to meet her. That certainly wasn't the reaction she'd been expecting.

Silas interrupted her confusion by asking his grandfather if his grandmother was home. Samuel said she was out to lunch with some friends to celebrate her birthday. Silas let him know he'd come to bring her a birthday gift, then explained the situation that he and Leah faced at the nearby store. "I was hoping Leah could relax here while I run back to get her *gaul* and buggy that are still at the store."

"Ach du lieva!" Samuel exclaimed, clutching his chest. "The Lord was certainly keeping his loving eye on both of you." He took the shopping bag from Silas, then set his hoe on the ground. "You can certainly rest here, Leah. *Kumme* into the *haus* with me, and we'll have ourselves a glass of meadow tea."

Silas thanked his grandfather and then set off on foot in the direction of Eby's Store.

Once she and Samuel were seated at the small oak table in the *dawdi haus*'s tiny kitchen, each with a tall glass of chilled meadow tea, Leah found the courage to ask the question that had been on her mind since meeting Silas's grandfather.

"Forgive me for being n-nosy, but I was w-wondering what you meant when you said you've been w-waiting years to meet me. Has Silas t-told you about me?"

Samuel sipped his tea and leaned back in

his chair. "I don't suppose it's a secret that our Silas wasn't always on the straight and narrow. Did he ever tell you about the night that he drove his truck into one of the trees on the edge of this property?"

"*Jah*, he m-mentioned that," Leah answered. She relished the refreshing beverage Samuel provided her, the cool drink helping to soothe her rattled nerves. "He didn't go into great d-detail, though."

Samuel rubbed the top of his head where his gray hair had thinned significantly. "After Silas sobered up and we were sure he wasn't injured, he and I had ourselves a real direct conversation. Seeing that he almost got himself killed, I felt it was important to remind him that life on earth is short, and he was dangerously close to cutting it even shorter."

Leah pondered that as she fiddled with the hem of her apron, frayed and torn from when she landed on the pavement when Silas pulled her out of harm's way. "Seems like a person doesn't realize just how n-numbered our days can be." She glanced around the tidy kitchen, noticing an enticing aroma of cinnamon. "Was Silas receptive to what you t-told him?"

Samuel nodded. "Didn't think he would be, but he was. When I realized I had his attention, for what seemed like the first time ever,

I asked him if he'd be at peace with the way he lived his life if he would have passed away in that crash."

"What did he s-say?"

"He broke down and wept, then admitted that he wouldn't be at peace." Samuel's slight grin started to tremble. "It was then and there that he made the decision to commit his life to follow *Gott*. He was baptized into the Amish church later that year."

Leah blinked several times to keep yet another round of tears from spilling. "I'm so *hallich* that he made that ch-choice," she said after taking a moment to compose herself. "Even though it was a d-difficult lesson."

Samuel leaned forward and folded his hands on the table. "The most important lessons are usually the ones that we insist on learning the hard way. But it's *gut* to see that everything worked out, just as *Gott* intended."

Leah stared at Samuel quizzically and waited for him to say more.

"In that same serious conversation that we had following the crash, Silas got to talking about all of his regrets. And believe me, there were many, but one story stood out. He told me a story about a girl named Leah Fisher, who he teased relentlessly over a stuttering disorder. He told me about how poorly he'd treated her and would give anything to take back the years of cruelty." Samuel paused, leaning even closer to Leah as he took her hand in his. "I can very clearly recall him saying that if given the chance, he'd make sure that nothing ever hurt you again. And now, here you two are, a real handsome couple. Seems like *Gott* worked all things out, as He always does."

Leah sat in stunned silence, unable to restrain her tears. Hearing that Silas had made such a confession to his grandfather, when it would benefit him in no way, revealed his true nature. *I can trust Silas with my heart. I don't have to be afraid ever again. I can share my heart with the man I love.* Her joyful thoughts swirled together, overwhelming her with relief, thankfulness and elation. She felt herself slip free of a lifetime of restlessness and leeriness. Every wall she'd ever built around her heart suddenly crumbled to pieces.

"*Denki* so much for sh-sharing this with me," Leah finally managed to say, giving Samuel's gnarled hand a few quick squeezes. "You don't know how m-much this means to me."

Samuel chuckled as they released each other's hands. "Something tells me that the *baremlich* day you've been having so far is about to turn *wunderbaar*, and I'm *hallich* to be a part of it."

* * *

"*Denki* for going back to f-fetch Jolly and my buggy," Leah called to Silas as he brought the horse to a halt at the edge of the driveway. Feeling more energetic and hopeful than ever, she'd been waiting near the road for Silas's return after having politely declined Samuel's offer of a second glass of meadow tea.

"I was happy to do it." He beamed at her with admiration. "I hope you haven't been waiting out here too long. You were supposed to be resting."

She smiled, appreciating his concern for her. "I've got s-something on my mind that I'd like to discuss r-right away."

"Let me unhitch Jolly and get her something to eat and drink, and then you'll have my full attention." He gave her a winning grin and then clicked his tongue to get Jolly walking toward the barn.

Leah followed close behind her buggy, nearly bursting with anticipation.

Once Jolly was comfortably settled into one of the empty horse stalls with a large bucket of cool water and plenty of oats to munch on, Silas invited Leah to walk with him to the apple orchard on the other side of his family's enormous farm. "It's awful peaceful over there, and there'll be snacks hanging from the trees."

"Aren't you all tuckered out from the ordeal with J-Jolly, then walking back to Eby's?" Leah asked as she playfully planted her hands on her hips.

He shook his head, his gaze blissfully stuck on her. "I believe I just caught a second wind."

Leah giggled as the pair ambled out of the barn and down a well-worn dirt lane that ran adjacent to a field of golden cornstalks that stood several feet higher than both of their heads. She noticed the earthy farm scents mingling with the freshness of the autumn air. She couldn't remember ever taking the time to enjoy simple pleasures, like filling her lungs with fresh country air. Now that she was finally free from the past, she promised herself to take the time to smell the proverbial roses much more often.

"Did you have a *gut* time with my *grossdaddi*?" Silas asked, pleasantly interrupting her train of thought.

"*Jah*, and I can see wh-why he's so special to you," Leah said as she gently hovered her hand near the cornstalks, the dry leaves tickling her skin as they continued walking.

Silas brightened at her response. "I knew you would."

They continued walking past fields of cornstalks and soybeans until they arrived at a grove of apple trees that were spaced perfectly apart in even rows, their branches heavy with ripe, red apples.

"So, what did you talk about?" Silas questioned, his hands nearly brushing against Leah's as they strolled leisurely through the orchard. "Did he tell you about the *gaul* he once owned that would only walk when leaving the barn but would gallop at full speed when returning? That's his favorite story to share."

Leah shook her head. "He told me about the c-conversation you two had after your accident, and how it ch-changed your outlook on life."

Silas froze in place. "I see." He stood motionless for several seconds, then ducked beneath one of the apple trees. Pressing his back against the trunk, he slid to the ground. "It sounds *narrish* to say, but I'm awful *dankbarr* that the accident happened. It woke me up."

"I under-s-stand," Leah replied, having experienced her own awakening earlier that day. Following suit, Leah knelt down and crawled beneath the low branches to Silas's side, then sat close enough to him so that she could lean her head on his shoulder. "S-Suddenly, I'm awake too. I want you to start b-bringing your buggy rides back to my roadside stand."

Silas ran his fingers through the silky grass, a hint of hesitant hopefulness causing his cheeks to flinch. "Really?"

"Jah." Leah put her hand on top of Silas's, stopping it from combing through the green wisps. "Your *grossdaddi* told me how you f-felt a need to protect me."

"I still feel that way," Silas assured her in a low voice. He leaned closer to her as a gentle breeze rustled his sandy blond hair.

"I think if I hadn't been so w-worried about protecting myself, I might have realized this s-sooner," she admitted, moving herself even nearer to him. "I won't ever let m-myself be anxious ever again, now that my heart has found her m-match."

Silas gently caressed the side of Leah's face, his loving eyes moving toward her lips. *"Ich lieb dich*, Leah. I want to spend my life with you. Will you be my bride, come this wedding season?"

Leah's heart soared above the apple trees and landed among the fluffy clouds. "I love you too, Silas. Nothing would make me happier than becoming your *fraa*."

Silas glowed at the declaration of her love and promptly gathered her into his adoring embrace. "My precious Leah, you didn't stutter once."

Leah giggled against his chest, fully relaxing into the peace that enveloped her. She closed her eyes, savoring the sweetness of her beloved's kiss, as well as each tender kiss that followed, knowing in her heart that this newfound joy and peace would last the rest of her life.

Epilogue

One Month Later

"Did you find everything you were looking for today?" Leah asked her *Englisch* customer as the woman brought an apple pie and two loaves of bread to the counter.

"I did." The woman smiled as she placed her purchases on the counter and reached into her purse for her wallet. "I always visit your place when I'm in Lancaster County. I'm coming back next week with some girlfriends, so I'll be sure to bring them here."

Leah grinned, pleased to serve such a loyal, frequent customer. "Thank you for your business. I'm sorry to disappoint you, but the shop will be closed next week." She gave the woman her total and started to place the baked goods into a paper shopping bag.

"Oh? Are you closing for a holiday that your community celebrates, or maybe you're doing some renovations?" the woman asked as she placed her payment on the counter.

Leah was flooded with so much happiness that she was nearly tickled pink. "We're closing just for the week because I'll be getting married on Thursday, and my family is hosting the wedding here on our farm."

"That's so exciting! Congratulations!" The woman squealed as she accepted her change from Leah. "Maybe we'll put off our trip a week so we can stop by when you've reopened."

Leah thanked the woman for her kind words and handed her the shopping bag. They said a short goodbye and the woman headed for the exit just as Silas entered the small shop.

"Another satisfied customer?" he asked with a loving grin.

Leah chuckled. "I don't want to brag, but I'd say she was quite satisfied." She leaned over the counter to peer out the nearby window. "Where are your buggy ride customers? Are they playing with Willow?"

"*Nee*, I came here by myself. I'm on a lunch break," he replied as he slipped behind the counter and gave Leah a quick peck on the cheek.

"If you skipped a meal just to see me, you

must really like me," Leah teased as she gave him a playful swat.

"*Jah*, I do," Silas beamed as he pulled her into his arms. "*Ich lieb dich*, Leah Fisher. Even more than mint chocolate whoopie pies."

Leah chuckled and snuggled against her future husband's chest, feeling content, safe, and loved. "Just think, in less than a week, we'll be *mann* and *fraa* and you'll be moving into our *haus*." She looked up at him as the tiniest bit of concern crept into her heart. "Will you mind going to your parents' place every day to continue running the buggy rides?"

"*Nee*, not at all, *mei lieb*." Silas reassured her, as he took both of her hands in his. "Plus, it won't be that way for long. Ivan and I will work on building a guest area here, and then Riehl's Buggy Rides will move to this farm." He let out a small laugh. "What a destination this place will be, *jah*? Farm tours, a roadside stand and buggy rides all in one spot. What more could anyone visiting Lancaster County want?"

Leah bobbed her head in agreement. "I'm so *dankbarr* that you had the idea to unite our businesses, even though I was less agreeable when you first brought up the idea." She felt her eyes starting to water with joyful tears. "Everything worked out according to *Gott*'s perfect plan when I finally put my trust in Him." She wrapped her arms around Silas's neck and gazed into his eyes. "*Denki* for being so patient with me as I learned to fully trust the Lord."

"I'd wait until the end of time for you, Leah," Silas replied softly, his eyes shining with love. "But I'm glad I don't have to wait so we can start our lives together now."

He leaned closer to her, and their lips met in a kiss that was sweeter than any of the cookies that were for sale in Leah's Countryside Cupboard.

* * * * *

Dear Reader,

If you find yourself driving along the scenic backroads of Lancaster County, you're likely to come across dozens of Amish roadside stands. Some of these special locations are simple sheds that only sell fresh-picked produce on the honor system, while others have grown into impressive establishments.

My favorite roadside stand is located just a few miles from Bird-in-Hand. I love to browse through the selection of homemade items that are for sale, including baked goods, quilts, crafts, toys and soaps. There's something peaceful about visiting a business on an Amish farm. I can't help but think of how fulfilling it must be to tend to the little shop and interact with all of the visitors who are looking to take home a piece of Amish Country.

That's how the idea for Leah's story was born! I hope you enjoyed falling in love with Leah and Silas as much as I did.

I'd love to hear from you! Connect with me on my Facebook page, Jackie Stef's Plain & Fancy.

Blessings and Peace,
Jackie Stef

Get 3 FREE REWARDS!

We'll send you 2 FREE Books _plus_ a FREE Mystery Gift.

FREE
Value Over
$20

Both the **Love Inspired®** and **Love Inspired® Suspense** series feature compelling novels filled with inspirational romance, faith, forgiveness and hope.

HARLEQUIN PLUS

Try the best multimedia subscription service for romance readers like you!

Read, Watch and Play.

Experience the easiest way to get the romance content you crave.

Start your **FREE TRIAL** at
www.harlequinplus.com/freetrial.